MUDROOM MYSTIC

MAGICAL RENOVATION MYSTERIES BOOK SEVEN

AMY BOYLES

LADYBUGBOOKS LLC

Mudroom Mystic

A MAGICAL RENOVATION MYSTERY • BOOK 7

AMY BOYLES

CHAPTER 1

"What are you doing?" I asked, watching as Malene Fredericks, my grandmother, placed what must have been the fiftieth garden gnome in her front yard.

She straightened him in the dirt with a huff and glared up at me. "What does it look like I'm doing?"

"Going crazy," I replied.

She pressed her lips into a sour frown. "For your information, I am decorating my yard."

"With a thousand garden gnomes?"

"That's correct."

"Why?"

She flared out her skinny arms and arched them together as if she was going to hug someone, but stopped short. "Because the garden gnome competition is two days away, and I plan to win."

This was the first I'd heard of such a thing. "Garden gnome competition?"

She sniffed the air. "That is correct."

"I don't think that exists."

My dog, Lady, who'd been sniffing grass down the street, padded up to us. She took one look at the minefield of red-hatted gnomes and broke out into barking. "Who are you looking at? I'll punch you right in the throat! Stay back, tiny bearded men, or else I'll bite your heads off."

I leaned down and patted her back. Lady jumped and snapped at me. "Whoa, Trigger," I soothed. "Those gnomes can't hurt you. They're inanimate objects."

"I don't care if they're inanimate *animates*," she bit back. "Them's some creepy little men."

I stifled a laugh as Malene's face turned bright pink. "Sorry, Malene. Lady's not used to seeing so many garden gnomes."

Lady stretched her nose forward and sniffed one of the tiny men that stood frozen, smiling into the distance. "Don't you think having so many of them all together will spread diseases? Do they come to life at night and tinkle all over the yard?"

I barked a laugh. "Lady, they're made of porcelain. They don't come to life."

She glanced at me skeptically. "Says you."

Malene curled both her hands into fists and cemented them to her hips. "If all the two of y'all are going to do is criticize my lawn ornaments, you can leave."

"Malene, I'm sorry." And I did my best to sound like I meant it, too. "It's just that in all the time I've lived here, I don't remember a gnome competition."

"We took a break from it," she explained. "On account that there was a gnome shortage for a while."

I arched a brow. "A gnome shortage?"

"Yeah, they were using up all the porcelain in England to make the gnomes so we couldn't get any this far south. You know, gnomes aren't as popular here as they are over in Europe. They like their gnomes. So we had to put the contest on hold. But now we've got the gnomes back and I'm happy to say that I think my yard looks good. I might actually win this year."

Well, if the previous winners had been lawns that looked like they'd vomited gnomes, then Malene was definitely in the lead.

"The only person I have to worry about is Gilbert Wilcox."

I arched a brow. "Gilbert Wilcox?"

Malene scurried around, adjusting statue after statue—righting some and moving others. "Every year Gilbert wins the contest. I don't know how he does it. He doesn't have a ton of gnomes, but what he does have, he uses to his advantage."

"You're making him sound like a beauty pageant contestant," I joked.

Malene looked at me with dead serious eyes. "If there was a beauty contest in town, Gilbert Wilcox would sure as heck be one of the top three. That man has more fashion sense than a red carpet model. He can take a scarf and drape it over a lamp, thereby changing the whole feel of room. I don't know how he does it."

Lady stopped chewing a clump of grass and answered, "Sounds like he just throws a scarf on a lamp. That's how he does it."

Malene swatted at her impatiently. "I know *how* he does it. I just don't know *how* he does it."

Lady glanced up at me perplexed. "Didn't she just say the same thing?"

"Yes," I murmured.

In the house beside us, the front door opened with a bang, and my grandfather, Willard Gandy, appeared. He took one look at Malene's yard and slapped his face.

"Malene, don't tell me it's that time of year again, is it?"

Malene adjusted her dark round Jackie O glasses. "Okay, I won't tell you it's that time of year again. But get ready, because I'm going to need your yard. I ordered fifty more gnomes, and they're due here any day now."

Willard stormed down the front steps. "Don't tell me you plan on putting them on my grass."

"Okay, I won't tell you that." My grandmother pointed a bony finger, swollen at the knuckles, at him. "But I'll need you to bring your wheelbarrow out front because I'm going to dump a couple of gnomes in it."

"Malene, now it's one thing for you to decorate your own lawn. It's quite another for you to"—he gestured wildly as he searched for the right word—"destroy my yard while you try to beat Gilbert Wilcox for the golden gnome."

Lady and I exchanged a look. *A golden gnome?* Now I'd heard everything.

Just then a car horn beeped the beginning of "Amazing Grace" up through the "how sweet the sound" part. I glanced behind me to see a convertible cyan Cadillac, circa 1960-something, slow down as it neared Malene's.

Her eyes narrowed to slitty wedges of death. "Gilbert Wilcox," she muttered bitterly.

The infamous Gilbert Wilcox came to a stop. He had a round face and even rounder body. One meaty hand clutched the steering wheel as if he was out on a leisurely cruise of Peachwood. His blond hair was oiled back, and a pencil mustache dusted his upper lip. A red scarf was tucked into the opening of his shirt, making him look quite debonair— in a 1940s sort of way.

"Why, Malene Fredericks," he said jovially, "I'm surprised to see you out and about quite so early. Getting ahead on decorating, are you?"

"I am," she said stiffly. "What are you doing, eyeing the competition? Cheating to make sure that you win this year?"

Gilbert threw his head back and laughed. "I assure you, I don't have to cheat in order to win. I'm hoping that I'll retain ownership of the golden gnome. But there are no guarantees."

"Humph," was all Malene managed.

Gilbert's gaze flicked to me. "And what's this? Are you recruiting help this year?"

"This is my granddaughter." Malene jerked her hand at Gilbert. "You keep your paws off her, Gilbert. She's got a boyfriend and he's tough. He could crush a gnome with his bare hands."

Oh, Lawd. How embarrassing.

"I see," Gilbert managed. "Well, how do you do? I'm Gilbert Wilcox, five-time golden gnome champion."

"Clementine Cooke," I replied, taking the clammy hand he offered. "And wow, five-time champion. You must work very hard."

Gilbert laughed bashfully. "Oh, it's not hard work to win around here."

Malene growled.

Gilbert's gaze darted to her. Seeming to realize his mistake, he sputtered. "I didn't mean that I don't have any competition. Not at all. The competition in Peachwood is fierce. Malene always gives me a run for my money. She's a tough cookie to beat."

Malene nodded in approval. "I work hard at it every year."

Gilbert lifted his nose and peered into the yard. "Looks like you've got a little bit of everything, don't you? Even kissing gnomes."

She did indeed have kissing gnomes. My grandmother also displayed fishing gnomes, sitting gnomes, napping gnomes, gnomes with their pants pulled down, biker gnomes, nudist sunbathing gnomes, gnomes sitting on toilets, and the list continued. There were so many gnomes it was giving me a headache to look at them.

"I'm very proud of my collection," Malene chirped.

Gilbert nodded appreciatively. "Looks like you might have a shot of winning, as always."

He said the words flatly, as if he didn't believe them. Malene caught his tone, and a spark flared in her eyes. "What do you have going on in your yard this year?"

"Me?" He placed a hand delicately on his chest. "What do I have going on?"

Malene rolled her eyes. "Yes, you."

"Hopefully less than what you've got," Willard mumbled.

"Willard," Gilbert exclaimed, "I could barely see you with all those gnomes around. How've you been?"

"Fine until I woke up this morning to this mess." My grandfather raked his fingers through his hair. "I don't know why it is, but this time of year always sneaks up on me."

"You and me both," Gilbert said innocently. But the gleam in his eye suggested otherwise. No one could be a five-time golden gnome champion and not have a strategy for how to win the trophy. "But I tell you, this year I'm going simple."

Malene's brows shot to peaks. She stuttered as if the very idea struck fear in her heart. "S-simple? You're going simple?" She clutched the convertible's passenger door. "What do you mean?"

Gilbert waved a hand in the air dismissively. "Oh, you know. I'm taking it easy."

"I don't believe you," she said.

He chuckled. "Don't believe it if you wish, but I promise you that you won't see a grand display from me."

Malene leaned over so far her nose nearly touched his. "So there won't be any waterfall of gnomes?"

"Nope," he said.

"No gnomes tumbling down the hill and spilling onto the sidewalk?"

"No."

"Any gnomes dancing on your roof?"

"Not that either."

"How about gnomes pushing up out of their graves?"

What?

Gilbert yawned. "No, no and no. I told you. I'm going simple. I'm not doing all of that mess."

Malene eyed him skeptically. "I'll buy it when I see it."

Willard fired out, "Malene, if the man said he's not doing all of that, then he's not doing it."

Malene jabbed her finger in Gilbert's face. "You've got a plan to win. I know you, Gilbert. You're scoping out the competition. You're coming here and making me think you're going easy so that I'll believe I don't have to work as hard. I don't buy it. You'll probably put out as many gnomes as you normally do and are just trying to trick me. Well it won't work. I know your kind, with your beady eyes and shuffling gaze. Your lying don't fool me."

She spat out the last sentence and folded her arms for emphasis. We stood in silence. Even Lady had stopped chewing grass and stared at Malene, mouth agape.

Willard clapped his hands. "Malene, why don't you come inside? It's getting hot out here, and you could use a glass of sweet tea."

"I don't need a glass of sweet tea," she said coldly.

"You sure? You're getting awfully *hangry*. You get that way when your blood sugar drops. You could use some calories."

Willard was practically pleading, but Malene wasn't budging. She poked Gilbert right in the throat. "What are you up to?"

He laughed. "I'm not up to anything, Malene Fredericks. I was just driving by and practically telling you that I was going easy on my gnomes this year, and you're accusing me of lying."

"That's because you are."

The words hung heavily in the air. No one moved. I swear that no one even breathed. I know that I didn't. I held my breath until my lungs burned. It was then and only then that I exhaled.

Willard murmured, "Oh no. Now she's done it."

And she had done it. Gilbert Wilcox's face turned the color of a bright pink azalea. He glared at Malene and announced, "Well, I *was* going to go easy, but you, Malene Fredericks, have pushed me over the edge. All I did was stop by for a friendly chat. But I see that you cannot deal with losing. So I am going to make sure that you lose the golden gnome for a fifth year in a row!"

With that, Gilbert hit the gas and sped off down the street, his tires squealing and the scent of burning rubber filling the air.

Malene brushed her hands. "I think that went well. What about y'all?"

She glanced over, waiting expectantly for my answer. How had it gone? Well, my grandmother had succeeded in ticking off her main competition for the gnome contest. She'd called him a liar and pretty much embarrassed herself and us. How had it gone? It had gone terribly.

But saying that wouldn't help anything. So I grinned widely and replied in my most pleasant voice, "Would you look at the time? I've got a house to get to. Sorry that I can't stay and chat. Lady, we'd better get going."

She stared blankly at me. "You didn't say anything about leaving."

I laughed nervously under Malene's laser-focused stare. "Didn't I? Well, sorry that I forgot to say anything earlier. But we need to get to the new house. I've got some… um…some finishes to pick out."

Malene's voice became gravelly. "If I didn't know better, I'd say you were skirting around the question."

I scoffed. "Who? Me? Never. But listen"—I started to back away—"the gnomes look great. I'll see you soon. Willard, I think the decorations will look fabulous when they come in. See y'all later."

With that, I grabbed Lady and crossed the street, narrowly managing to avoid Malene's line of fire.

CHAPTER 2

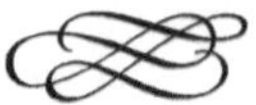

"And so you're saying that she planted a field of garden gnomes in her yard?" Rufus asked.

I laughed behind my hand. "Yes, and she wasn't finished yet. There are still more to put out. At least that's what she told me."

My boyfriend—or boy toy, as I liked to think of him to no one but myself—leaned his shoulder against a doorframe of my newly purchased home.

No, I wasn't moving. My plan was to flip this baby and perhaps make a little profit while I was at it.

Rufus's mouth broke into an amused smile. "There are more gnomes? More than what you've already said she has displayed?"

"Oh, so many more. Malene said she was expecting another truckload."

Rufus raked his fingers down his face. "Now I've heard it all. It wasn't enough that she decorated her own yard. She's going to plant gnomes in Willard's as well?"

"That is correct."

"She may even put some on the roof," Lady chirped as she strutted around the house, sniffing every possible corner. "She didn't say as much, but I swear that woman was thinking it."

Rufus chuckled. "I think that I can die a happy man if I see this spectacle."

"Why's that?" I asked.

"Because you make it sound like one of the seven wonders of the world. It comes right after the leaning tower of Pisa. Malene's yard, riddled with garden gnomes." He laughed. "And I suppose she's talked you into hosting some of the gnomes?"

"Heaven's no. Lady and I escaped as quickly as we could."

"Speak for yourself," Lady said. "You were the one who couldn't get out of there fast enough. You were practically running for higher ground."

I rolled my eyes. "Anyway."

Rufus's gaze held mine. "Anyway."

We stared at one another as the friction between us thickened. He gave me a warm smile that touched his eyes. Rufus reached out his hand, and I took it, relishing the goose bumps that pricked my skin all the way to my shoulder.

"Anyway," he repeated. "It's good to see you. It's been a few days."

"Feels like a lifetime," I murmured.

"It does, in fact."

We stepped toward the other, only stopping a hair's breadth apart. Rufus swept a hand up my cheek and into my hair. He pulled me to him and pressed his lips gently to mine. The slow kiss deepened, sending waves of want all the way to my toes.

We parted when Lady cleared her throat. "Get a room, you two."

Rufus's cheeks reddened with embarrassment. "Right. Well, then. What are we doing today?"

But my head still swam from his kiss. His words made no sense. "Um. What?"

He nodded to the house. "Here. What are we doing?"

Well, all I wanted to do was find a room. But apparently my dog wasn't going to let that happen. I slowly untangled myself from his arms. "Oh, right. That. Well, I wanted to ask you what you thought about some of the finishes I'm considering, and then we need to shore up the subfloor in the kitchen. It's sagging."

"Good thing I brought my tools," he said with a wink.

Wait. Was that a euphemism? When Rufus said the word *tools*, was he referring to something else?

I decided to play along. "Tools? You brought your tools, huh?" I said this while I rubbed my hand up and down his arm. "Are you going to show me your tools?"

"Absolutely." He clapped his hands, and a toolbox dropped into the middle of the room. "My tools. There's nothing fancy in there—hammer, screwdriver, a handsaw, some screws and nails, a level—you know, the essentials I need for this job."

Oh. So he really *had* meant tools. Bummer. Well, that was okay. I could work with that.

He opened the box and took out his saw—which, by the way, was electric and could not possibly fit in the box without the use of magic, which Rufus had bounds of. He was, in fact, the most magical person that I knew. He would probably argue the fact and say that I had more magic than him.

But between you and me—he was just being nice.

"Now." As he held the saw, I couldn't help but admire the bulge in his bicep. How strong he was. Like, really strong and muscular. "Show me exactly where I need to work."

"Oh, I'll show you where you need to work, all right."

He shot me a quizzical look, and I nearly slapped a hand over my mouth.

Rufus was here to do a job, and all I wanted to do was find the nearest dark room with him. If I kept making innuendos, he would wonder what was wrong with me.

In fact, I was beginning to wonder that.

Wait. No I wasn't. I was a living, breathing human being. One with needs, in fact. I had serious needs. And wants. I had lots of wants.

In fact, my "wants" was staring at me right now.

"Are you feeling all right?" Rufus asked.

I laughed and waved away his concern. "Of course. I feel fine. Great, actually. Well, what are we waiting for? Let me show you the soft spot."

While Rufus worked on the kitchen, I pulled the finishing samples from my bag and placed them on the countertop. It was an old, Formica-laden structure that would soon be replaced with hopefully something more along the lines of quartz.

I spent some time playing with various combinations and listening to the sounds of Rufus working. Within half an hour all the sawing and hammering finished and he appeared in the doorway, shirt off.

His abs were cut from diamonds. His stomach was flat and…perfect, rising just above the line of his hip bones. *Hip bones.* I saw hip bones.

I might die.

My jaw hit the floor. "Um, um…is everything okay?"

He raked his fingers through his hair, completely unaware that I was staring at him so hard I was surprised that laser beams weren't shooting from my eyes.

"All done," he said proudly. "It didn't take nearly as long as I thought."

I quirked a brow. "Did you use magic?"

"I may have a bit, yes."

"You cheated."

"No, I wouldn't say that. You never told me that I couldn't use magic." He sat on a stool and exhaled. "Besides, I wasn't at the right angle to hammer in some of the nails. So. Magic."

I laughed as I crossed to the fridge and pulled out one of the many bottles of water I kept stocked at the house, or cottage, I should say.

I purchased the home a few weeks earlier, sight unseen except for what I'd viewed online. It was a cozy three bedroom, one bathroom with bones that could hold up a tank. Really, the frame of the house was solid. It had two fireplaces—one in the living room and one in the master bedroom. My plan was to knock out one of the bedrooms, turn that into a master bathroom and add on a deck off the kitchen. The kitchen would be updated, along with the other existing bathroom. It would take a little bit of time. But Rufus had said he would help as much as possible. Heck, he'd already helped a lot by working on that floor. My next project would be to start on the new master bath.

I handed him the water. "Thank you," he said.

I let my fingers brush against his for longer than necessary before murmuring, "You're welcome."

I stared at his beautiful face and chest as he drank the water. He glanced over at me, a question in his eyes, and I quickly glanced away, heat flooding my cheeks.

But then I thought about it. Why was I turning away from him?

Rufus was hot. He was my boyfriend. I wanted to spend time with him —snuggly, warm, comforting time. If things moved on from cuddles and kisses to something more—so be it.

He finished his water and placed the bottle down with a satisfied sigh. "So refreshing."

"Good." I edged closer. "I'm glad."

He glanced up at me. His long eyelashes brushed his cheekbones. I couldn't help but nibble my bottom lip nervously as I leaned over and kissed him.

It was the same as before—starting slowly and building with pressure. I skimmed my fingertips over his biceps, up his shoulders. My hands made their way around his neck. A moan of pleasure escaped his lips and mine.

This was good. Rufus was reinforcing what I knew to be true. We wanted one another.

Our kiss broke, and he gazed hungrily into my eyes. "You're so beautiful."

"Thank you," I said shyly. "You're incredibly handsome—especially with your shirt off."

His lip crooked seductively. "Is that right?"

"That's right." I hedged before asking, "Maybe we could take ourselves back to my place."

He stiffened. "Well, I'm very sweaty, and all that manual labor probably has made me smell very, very bad."

I sniffed. "Nope. You smell great to me."

Rufus slowly unwound my arms from his neck. "I assure you that I'm not fit company in the state I'm in."

"You seem very fit to me." I ran a finger across his pecs. "Quite so, in fact."

He took my hand in both of his and rose. "I need to clean up. But maybe we can have dinner tonight? Or stargaze? There's supposed to be a meteor shower that we can see from town. We could probably watch from your roof, in fact. I'll bring a picnic and we can have one while we wait for the meteors."

"To serenade us?" I asked.

"Um, yes. Something like that," he said tactfully.

What was going on? My powers of seduction weren't making a dent on Rufus. They should have been. Shouldn't they?

I mean, here I was, a hot-blooded woman kissing a hot-blooded man. He should have jumped at my offer to take things to the next level.

Why wasn't he?

Was there something wrong with me? Fear set in. Maybe Rufus wasn't as into me as I thought. Maybe my charms were waning on him. Perhaps he didn't care about me as much as I thought.

He gently tapped my chin with his knuckles. "Let me get my shirt and toolbox and I'll walk you to your truck."

"Sounds great," I said, forcing my voice to sound chipper.

I showed him the samples quickly, and he gathered his things. We made our way to the vehicles, and I stood beside my truck with the words *Magical Renovations* etched on the side. My old pickup was the best calling card I had. I patted it on the side as Lady stopped at my heels.

I dropped my bag in the passenger seat and turned to Rufus, tipping my chin up to him as I waited for him to either kiss me or tell me that he loved me.

We'd said it several times. It wasn't anything new. And I needed it right now. I didn't know why I felt so raw, so unbelievably insecure about his feelings for me. It made no sense. But I did. I absolutely felt like I'd offered him something—namely me—and he hadn't taken that offer.

What sort of boyfriend was he, anyway?

Just kidding. He was the great kind. One who loved and cared for me.

Right?

He tucked a strand of hair behind my ear and smiled. "I'll come over around seven. How does that sound?"

"Perfect." I leaned toward him a little bit, jutting out my chest so that he knew I was willing to be kissed deeply. "It sounds like a great time."

He smiled and it was like the heavens opened. His dark eyes shone brightly. His teeth glimmered in the sunlight. I only hoped I looked as good to him as he did to me. This was it. We were gonna kiss, maybe a little hot and heavy. He'd come back to my place, and…eventually we'd make it to the roof.

I could see it all now. We'd eat fried chicken and giggle atop the blanket I'd spread out. I'd be wearing one of his T-shirts. No one could see me up on the roof because of the way the pitch was, and Rufus would be shirtless. After the meteor shower, we'd go back inside and snuggle (and possible other stuff) under the covers.

It would be a perfect night.

"I'll see you then," he said before kissing me on the cheek and stepping back. "Drive safely."

I could not help that my jaw dropped. That was it? There was no passionate kiss? No looking deeply into my eyes? No telling me that he loved me?

What the heck?

But the only response I could give him, the only one that allowed me to keep my dignity, was to smile brightly and say, "See you then. Don't be late. I'm sure I'll be hungry."

With that, I scooped Lady into the truck and we rumbled off, heading toward home. I could lie and tell you that everything was fine with me. But it was not. Disappointment sat heavy on my chest, and I worried that the rest of the night would only lead to more.

Well, I'd find out in a few hours, now wouldn't I?

CHAPTER 3

"Why're you wearing that sundress if you're going on top of the roof?" Lady asked. "Aren't you afraid that you'll get it dirty?"

I cut up lettuce while she watched me from the floor. "No, I'm not worried about this dress. That's what Shout stain remover is for."

My dog eyed me skeptically. You know, it is funny the looks dogs get on their faces. You might wonder what they mean. At least I used to until my dog started speaking. Then I didn't have to wonder anymore. I had front-row seats to the crazy that came out of her mouth.

Trust me, sometimes I wanted to lock that crazy right on up and never let it out.

"But it's such a pretty shade of yellow. You get up there on that roof, Clem, and you're sure to get a smudge on it."

I opened a bag of shredded carrots and dropped them atop the lettuce. "It'll be fine."

She eyed me, deep in doggy thought. "You are very particular about your clothes. You wear the old ones for getting dirty, not the nice ones. Normally you'd be wearing jeans and a checkered shirt to go up on top of a roof. But you're dressed nicely." Then she gasped in realization. "You plan on doing the nasty with Rufus—my soon-to-be stepdaddy! That's what you're aiming at."

I shrugged. There was no point denying it. Yes, I did plan on luring Rufus into my bedroom. Or heck, I might not even have to do any luring. We might have so much fun on that roof that he tore my clothes off me up there.

No, I was not an exhibitionist. I was not going to let a whole bunch of folks, including my grandparents, see me without a stitch of clothing on. If things started getting a little hot up on the roof, we'd make our way back into the house.

Probably.

To Lady I replied, "I will neither deny nor confirm your theory."

"You ain't got to deny or confirm it 'cause I know the truth! You're going to bed that man."

I grabbed a container of cherry tomatoes from the fridge and closed the door with a swing of my hips. "What Rufus and I do in the privacy of my bedroom is our business and no one else's."

"It is my business. I am involved in this family, too. Also, I sleep in your room. What am I supposed to do—watch?"

"Oh, that is disgusting," I dropped the tomatoes atop the greens and carrots. "No, you're not supposed to watch. You can sleep in another room—like the living room. You have a little bed in there."

Her eyes widened with fear. "Then you'll subject me to listening to you! Oh, Clem, it's too much. My fragile doggy demeanor can't handle all of that. First, I might see y'all in the act, and now I'll have to listen to all of it? What are you trying to do? Give me a heart attack?"

"How did you ever guess?" I teased.

She shot me a hard look. "That's not funny."

"Course it isn't funny." I dropped to my knees and smoothed my hand over Lady's ruffled scalp. "Listen, the last thing that I'm trying to do is add stress to your life. I don't want that. But at the same time, you have to understand that at some point things will progress with me and Rufus. They'll move on the path where physical things will happen in our relationship. That's just how it is. I'm sorry if that upsets you, but it's nature. If you weren't fixed, you'd be all over this."

"If I wasn't fixed, I'd be wearing diapers," she snapped.

"That is true. Trust me. I did you a favor. No babies, no diapers, and all the dog food you could ever dream of. You're living the life, if you ask me."

She tipped her nose to the ceiling. "I don't call listening to the passion of my caregiver living the life."

I laughed and scratched her head. "Then put your head under a pillow."

"I am a dog! We can hear better than we can see."

"Oh, right." I surveyed the salad and decided it needed olives. I took them from the fridge and sprinkled a few on top. "Well, how about I magic up some ear wax and you can stick it in your ears?"

"I don't have thumbs! How am I supposed to plug them up?"

She had a point and a good one at that. "Well, I guess we're at an impasse."

Lady cocked her head. "What's that mean?"

"It means that we don't have a solution." With the olives the salad was perfect. I covered it in plastic wrap and put it away to chill. When done, I brushed my hands and turned to Lady, who still stared at me, waiting for her problems to be solved. "Okay. So. You can't do earplugs. You can't put your head under a pillow. I know. Why don't you stay with Malene tonight?"

She considered this. I know that because my dog got her thinking look on her face. After a few moments she asked, "Do you believe that's far enough away that I won't hear what y'all're up to?"

"Lawd, I hope so. If you can still hear me across the street, then that should mean something is going very, very right."

Lady rolled her eyes.

"Just kidding," I said. But I wasn't. If my doggy heard the throes of passion from way over at Malene's, then things were going good for me, if I did say so myself. "Come on. Let's go ask Malene if you can stay with her."

"Why don't you just call her?"

"Because," I said, picking up her bag of dog food, "if I show up with you, she's more likely to take you in. If I just call and ask, she might say no. Let's go."

Malene answered her door wearing all black. Like, it was summer and here she was dressed in a black long-sleeved turtleneck and black polyester pants. Just looking at her in all that heavy dress made me want to start scratching myself. I don't know what it was, but whenever

I even got a glance of a sweater during the heat of summer, I wanted to die.

"Why're you dressed like that?" I asked.

"Like what?"

"Like it's February."

My grandmother glanced down at herself. "I don't know what you're talking about. I always wear this."

"In July," I said, doubt thick in my voice.

"In July," she confirmed.

"Right. Okay, well, I was wondering if you'd be so kind to take Lady tonight? I've got plans, and well, she doesn't want to be around."

Malene smirked. "You got a hot date, huh?"

"And I don't want to hear the throes of passion," Lady chirped. "I might never recover."

"What is wrong with you?" I asked my dog. "Do you have to tell everyone my business?"

"Malene already guessed that you've got a hot date," Lady quipped. "It wouldn't have taken her long to figure out that you're dumping me on her so that you can have sexy time with Rufus."

"Shh," I snapped. "I don't want the entire neighborhood to know."

Malene winked at me deviously. "If everything goes well, they'll find out anyway."

"Sheesh, y'all. Look, Lady, it was one thing discussing all of this with you. But we do not need to drag my grandmother into this."

Lady's jaw dropped. "You just did when you brought me over here."

Okay, I was done with this. I tossed Lady's leash into Malene's hands. "Will you please watch my dog tonight?"

She sniffed. "What if I have plans?"

I gestured to her outfit. "What? You got a funeral in Alaska or something?"

"It's none of your business."

I folded my arms and glared at her. "Will you, or won't you? Or do I need to get Willard over here and ask him to watch her because apparently you've got some sort of secretive stuff going on."

Her gaze darted quickly over to Willard's. "No, that won't be necessary. I'll keep Lady. We'll make popcorn and watch old movies. Maybe there's a good Hitchcock marathon on tonight."

"Great. Lady"—I softened my voice—"you have a good time, and I'll pick you up first thing in the morning."

She wagged her tail. "Don't be too early. I'd like Malene to make us pancakes."

"Pancakes'll constipate you."

"It's a small price to pay for happiness," my dog said as she crossed the threshold.

"And Malene, try to stay out of trouble."

My grandmother's eyes widened in shock. "Well of course I'll stay out of trouble. I've never been in trouble in all my life."

"Right." I rolled my eyes. "See y'all tomorrow."

Malene winked. "Maybe you'll be glowing."

I hoped so. But I wasn't about to give her the pleasure of knowing how I felt. After all, she might have been my grandmother, but Malene was also a sneaky dame if there ever was one.

"Have fun," Malene said.

"I intend to," I replied, walking away. Boy, did I intend to. I glanced at my watch. There was about thirty minutes before Rufus arrived, and I still had some work to do in the house. If everything went smoothly, this night would be filled with more than a meteor shower. It might end with a full-on fireworks display.

I giggled to myself. Yep, fireworks indeed.

CHAPTER 4

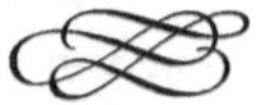

"*I* must say the view up here is spectacular," Rufus murmured as he helped me spread a blanket atop the roof. "Really, how'd you manage it?"

I shrugged noncommittally. "Oh, you know, it's just the pitch of the thing. It just happens to be a little higher than most of the others around."

And it was. The way my two-story cottage's roof had been constructed, it rose a little bit higher than the surrounding buildings, giving me a bird's-eye view of not only my block, but a couple of blocks away as well.

Not that I was going to use that advantage to become a Peeping Tom or anything. I never even went up on the daggum thing. But that could change if the roof got Rufus in the right mood. Heck, this could become my new favorite hangout.

He lifted a food box. "I brought chicken."

"And I made salad." I showed him the bowl. "Wait. I forgot plates."

He winked. "I think I can handle getting those." The next thing I knew, Rufus had magicked up utensils, napkins, plates and even a bottle of wine.

"Well, look at you." I extended my hand for him to take and help me down to a seated position. "You just thought of everything."

Red smeared his cheeks. "If that's a thank-you, I'll take it."

I glanced at him over my shoulder. "It is very much a thank-you. Now. I'm starving for both food and a meteor shower. I hope this show gets going soon."

He chuckled amiably and dished out fried chicken. "Tell me what you'd like—wing, thigh…"

"Breast," I said hoarsely. "I'll take the breast."

Was it just me or did his cheeks turn an even darker shade of red? Yep. They were almost plum-colored. Looked like I was doing my seducing job just fine.

He laid a gigantic chicken breast on my plate. There was no way in the world I'd be able to finish it. "Want to split it?"

"Absolutely." He set about slicing the meat in two and then settled one half on his own plate along with salad. "It's really nice up here. We should do this more often."

I eyed him demurely. "Yes, we should."

Our gazes locked, and I could feel the tension rising between us. It was almost hard to tell it apart from the Alabama humidity, but there was a real difference between sexual tension and just plain sultry. And this moment was thick with the first one.

"So," he started, "how long do you think it'll be before you have the house ready to sell?"

Was he avoiding my seductive glances and throaty words? I smiled. Rufus was not going to discourage me tonight. "I'm hoping to have it done in a few weeks. It shouldn't take too long with both of us working on it, and Liam said that he could help, too."

Liam was my construction manager on the paying jobs that I took. He was great—like a brother. Our relationship had always been completely platonic, and that was a good thing.

"I can help as much as you need," Rufus offered between bites of chicken.

"Oh?" I quirked a brow. "You don't have any spell hunting jobs outlined before you?"

"Surprisingly, no. Sykes Laffoon doesn't need me to hunt anything down for him."

Sykes Laffoon was head of the local wizard mafia. I know, I know. It made no sense. A wizard mafia? How was that even supposed to work?

Don't ask me. I had no idea. But Rufus had collected some spells for them in order to pay off a debt that my old business partner had accrued.

See? Rufus definitely loved me. Only someone who loved you would take on your debt. Why was I even questioning his feelings?

"To be honest, I'm almost a bit concerned," he admitted.

"Why? And wow, this chicken is so good. I don't know where you got it from, but I would gladly eat this again."

"I made it," he said proudly.

I lightly punched his shoulder. "You're kidding."

"I am not."

"Well, it's amazing. If you can cook Southern this good, what else can you do?"

He chuckled bashfully. "You could find out."

See? Innuendo right there. Okay, he was on this train with me. We were on the ride together. My chest unclenched. Seriously, I hadn't even realized that it was so tight. Now I could relax a little, take a load off.

Rufus and I were on the same wavelength.

This was good. It was very good.

I was openly staring at him, and Rufus cleared his throat, looking away. "Like I was saying, I'm a bit concerned that Sykes hasn't contacted me."

"Why?" I wiped grease from my fingers onto a napkin. "Wouldn't you want him to leave you alone so that you could hunt spells for other people?"

"Normally, yes. But if you recall, you had quite a time of it recently."

"You're talking about when I used a whole bunch of magic."

He nodded. "That would be correct."

"I don't see how that has anything to do with Sykes."

"Then you're not thinking hard enough."

I shot him a scathing look. "Are you trying to tick me off?"

"No, not at all. I'm only being honest. Sykes makes no bones about the fact that he works for someone else—someone no one knows. He has purchased spells from me in the past, but he hasn't lately. Why? Don't answer, because I will."

"Go for it," I said with a wink.

"I believe that whoever Sykes works for may have discovered the amount of power you displayed. If that's the case, then they may be looking directly at you and what you can do. They won't be interested in me anymore, unless it relates to your and my relationship."

"Our relationship?" I wiggled my brows. "And what is it exactly that they will think about our *relationship?*"

"Exactly what it is," he told me.

"Which is?"

He eyed me quizzically. "That I love you. Surely they'll know that. I would think that would be obvious to anyone around."

Finally. He said it. Great. Now we could get on to the good stuff.

"And that's why I'm worried. I think they're planning something."

I scoffed. "What could they be planning? What would they want with me? For all we know, what I did when it came to closing that portal was a fluke—a one-time deal."

Frustration filled his eyes. "It wasn't a fluke. No matter what you want to believe, the power stored in you, Clementine Cooke, is great. You could be a weapon for anyone who wants to use you. Surely you must see that."

I swatted him. "You're being way too serious about all of this. This is Peachwood. We have a little bit of crime. Sometimes strange magical things happen here, yes. But no one is going to be looking at me and thinking that I'm some great nexus of power." Rufus said nothing, which made a knot form in the back of my throat. I swallowed it down long enough to add, "Will they?"

"I don't know, and that's what worries me. Even Malene believes that your power, if it's discovered, could put you in danger."

"I don't think anyone will try to steal it, if that's what you're suggesting."

Darkness flashed in his eyes. It was a sore subject, the idea of stealing power, because not long ago Rufus had been the sort of wizard who wanted to do just that—take my gift.

I rubbed his leg. "Don't you worry. You're here to protect me, right? You won't let anyone get near me to do any damage like that."

He took my hand. Finally, some intimate contact. And if truth be told, I was a bit worried. For the past few weeks I had tried not to think about what had gone on in Norma Ray's barn. That the portal that gave a person whatever they asked for, had been closed—by me. But I had been worried. Oh, I'd shoved my fear aside and had thrown myself into the plans for my new house and now I was trying to jump Rufus's bones, but that was honestly just a distraction from what really bothered me—that someone I didn't want to find out that I had power, would.

Not that I knew exactly who that person was yet. But the boulder in my belly suggested that they were coming, and I was doing my darndest to distract myself before they reared their ugly head.

Rufus's fingers entwined with mine. "I will protect you no matter what. Whatever you need, I'm there. I'll make sure that you're safe and taken care of if it's the last thing that I do."

"No need to be so dramatic," I said shyly.

"I can't help it. You make me feel this way."

He leaned forward and kissed me. I melted onto him. *There.* That's what I'd been looking for. That was what I needed—some comfort. Yes, I could have just told Rufus that I was worried, but what would that have accomplished? I would have felt vulnerable, like a lost child.

I was not a child.

I was very much grown up.

As I could tell from the tingle coming from my girlie parts.

Our lips disconnected, and I immediately felt lost without them on mine. Rufus glanced up before breaking into a smile. "The meteor shower's starting."

What crappy timing. "Already? Great. Let's watch it."

I leaned my head on his shoulder and glanced up. Tails of light crashed through the sky. There were dozens of them. Rufus and I spent the next twenty minutes pointing to—and I swear—each and every meteor that speared across the sky.

I would have continued watching, too, if voices from Malene's house hadn't grabbed my attention. "What is going on over there?" I murmured, craning my neck to see better.

Because of the pitch of my roof, I had to rise and lean over a wedge of house in order to get a better look.

What was going on was that Norma Ray and Urleen, Malene's best friends, had showed up.

"Hurry up," Norma Ray shouted from Urleen's car. "We gotta get over there."

Malene crept down her front porch, still wearing all black and holding Lady under her arm.

"Where are they going?" I said.

"To a gnome party?" Rufus asked.

I elbowed him. "You know, you might actually be right."

"I think the judging's soon."

I shot him a surprised look. "How do you know when the judging is? Are you competing?"

"No, of course not. But I hear things in town." He rose and watched the scene unfold. "You can't help but hear things the way people get worked up about contests."

"Tell me about it."

"Do you want me to?"

I playfully nudged my shoulder against his. "I think that I'm okay."

"As you wish."

"But where are they going?"

Malene was in the vehicle now, and Urleen sped off, slowing only for the stop sign. She took a left and went to one more stop sign before taking another left. They stopped in front of a house that had its porch light on. It was then that I noticed there were gnomes sprinkled on that lawn, too.

I gasped. "Oh no."

"What do you mean, oh no?" Rufus asked.

"A million bucks says they're at Gilbert Wilcox's."

"Is that the man Malene ticked off?"

"Yes, it is." I craned my neck, trying to get a better look. "What could they be doing?"

But even without asking, I knew what Malene was up to. She was over at Gilbert's with only one intention—to sabotage the contest. She had convinced her friends and had even taken my dog to his home in order to wreck the gnomes.

"Come on," I said to Rufus.

He rose slowly. "You're not telling me that we're about to get involved."

"We most certainly are. We've got to stop Malene before she gets herself and my dog arrested."

CHAPTER 5

$\mathcal{A}$s much as I hated to leave the rooftop—and trust me, it pained me all the way to my core—I let Rufus help me down and into the house.

"Leave it to Malene," he murmured as we headed to the front door.

"What's that mean?" I slipped into a pair of sandals I kept near the entrance. "Are you blaming Malene for ruining our meteor date?"

He slid his warm palms over my cheeks in a move that made a shiver shimmy its way to my toes. "I hope that after we've finished stopping whatever catastrophe she's determined to create, we'll be able to pick up where we left off."

"That sounds like my kind of plan." And darn Malene for ruining what could be one of the greatest moments of my life. Or at least one of the greatest moments of the year. Tonight could have been the moment that shaped the rest of my life.

Wait. Did I want that?

Perhaps I should slow down a bit. Having Rufus over for the night was very different than deciding to spend the rest of my life with him. I was not quite there yet. Yes, I was ready to go some distance with him, but eternity? Well, perhaps I needed to just calm my girlie parts down a bit (they were in a tizzy) and think more with my brain than my hormones.

But if it did happen, if Rufus did pop *the question*, would I be up for it? I gazed into Rufus's eyes, into the kind soul that I knew he was, and realized, I would. I would be okay if he dropped to one knee in front of me and held out a ring.

Wow. Where had that come from?

I walked my fingers up Rufus's bicep. "Well, we'll just have to hope that this whole thing with Malene doesn't take too long. Come on, let's see what sort of craziness she's about to do."

We reached Gilbert's house a couple of minutes later. Don't ask me how I knew it was Gilbert's house. I guess it was just some sixth sense I had. Also, who else's gnome-covered yard would Malene have put under siege?

No one's, that was who.

The house was quiet when we arrived. The outside lights were off (I assume thanks to Malene), and Urleen had parked her car a little ways down. I had to say that even with the streetlamps illuminating small slashes of grass, it was obvious that Gilbert had a gift when it came to decorating with the gnomes. He didn't just scatter them as Malene had seemed to do. Oh no, Gilbert had style—and not only style, but also a game plan.

One cluster of gnomes were children playing jump rope. Then another were animatronic gnomes sliding into a swimming pool. There were gnomes playing in leaves and some in snow. That's when I realized Gilbert's theme—the four seasons.

"This is really good," I murmured to Rufus. "This man is a genius."

"He does have a way with gnomes," he agreed. "But where is Malene? I don't see her or her cohorts anywhere."

Where had she gone? My grandmother was not to be spotted in the front. "She must be around back. Let's go find her."

As we started to make our way to the back of the house, I heard Malene whisper very loudly, "Hurry up! Get that other gnome up here."

My gaze darted to the roof of all places, and there they were—Malene, Urleen, Norma Ray, and my dog. Malene gestured to the other two women in a quick, hurried fashion.

"Hurry up, he could be back any second," Malene demanded.

"This thing is heavy, Malene," Norma Ray shot back. "It's not so easy to pull up."

"I did it," my grandmother retorted. "And if I can do it, you can, too."

"Then you get your butt over here and do it."

Malene sniffed. "I'm upper management. I don't do grunt work."

"It is heavy, Malene. We could use another hand."

"It smells funny up here," Lady murmured. "I don't like it. Hey look, there's Clem. Hey, Clem!"

"Hey," I said warmly. No use making them suspicious by yelling at them right off the bat. "What're y'all doing up there atop Gilbert's roof? This is Gilbert's house, right?"

Malene froze. "We're not doing anything."

Urleen and Norma Ray shot her worried looks. I could see their faces because even though it was dark atop the house, all three of the women and my dog wore headlamps. Yes, headlamps.

"Perhaps you should come down before anyone gets hurt," Rufus said.

"Oh, we're not going to get hurt," Norma Ray said. "We've got lots of gnomes to keep us steady."

"Be quiet," Malene hissed. "They don't need to know what we're doing."

I folded my arms. "Malene, I suggest you get down here before you either break your neck or get arrested."

"I'm not getting arrested. I'm not doing anything illegal."

"I believe," Rufus said, "that what you're doing is considered trespassing. Yes, you could be arrested or, at the very least, detained. Perhaps you should come down before this, whatever it is, gets out of hand."

"Nothing is getting out of hand. See?" Malene flashed her palms. "I've got both hands right here."

"And she's also got a few booties," Norma Ray said jovially.

"Hush," Urleen said, fixing her glasses.

"What?" Norma Ray asked innocently. "Can't Clem know that we're going to moon the whole town?"

"Wonderful," Rufus muttered. He punched his hands in his pockets and stepped forward. "Ladies, as much as I hate to break up this wonderful nighttime revelry, I think it's time this came to an end. You're on private property about to sabotage this man's chances at winning the, um…" Rufus glanced at me for help.

"Golden gnome," I prompted.

"Really? They win a golden gnome?"

I shrugged. "Haven't you just about heard it all at that point?"

"I do believe I have." He smirked. "What will they think of next?"

"Golden Smurfs?"

"What is a Smurf?"

I waved away his question. "Never mind. Please continue. You were doing well, but now you've lost their attention."

Which was true. While Rufus had directed his questions to me, the women had been busy heaving gnomes into place.

Rufus shook his head. "I'm afraid they won't listen if I'm down here." He offered a hand, and I slid my palm atop his. "Would you care to join me on a roof for the second time tonight?"

"You know the third time's the charm," I said with a smile.

Warmth danced in his eyes. "It is. We may have to work that into this evening. But first"—his gaze darted up and down the street—"we'd better get up there before the police appear."

"Understood."

He winked. "Hold tight."

A burst of power surged from Rufus, entangling me like an octopus's tendrils. His magic pulsed in my body. It was a rush, like plunging into a pool of cold water. Before the shock was completely over, we stood atop the roof a little ways down from the women.

"Oh good," I said, looking down. "There's sort of a walkway up here. It would be hard to fall off."

Malene pursed her lips. "You kids act like I don't know what I'm doing. I'll have you know that I scouted the place before we came up here."

"I'm not sure if that's something you should be proud of," Rufus told her.

"Well I am sure," Malene retorted. "I'm proud of myself."

Rufus glanced back at me. "This is *your* grandmother."

"Please don't hold it against me."

He shook his head as if to say that he wasn't, and then Rufus clapped his hands. "Ladies, this is over. You've had your fun and games, but now it's time to stop this with the—oh my, are all those gnomes naked?"

Norma Ray lifted one of the gnomes proudly. "He's got a little winky."

"No comment." Rufus glanced at me for help. "Do you mind? I think I may actually be out of my scope of practice here."

I nibbled my bottom lip to keep from laughing and stepped around him. "Malene, I know what you're planning to do."

She raked her fingers through her coiffed hair. "What's that?"

"You plan to put the little fat gnomes on his roof so that Gilbert won't see them until it's too late—after the judging's already done."

"I have no idea what you're talking about," she snapped. "We were simply driving by and saw that some of his gnomes had fallen to the ground. So we came up here to fix them. Right, ladies?"

Urleen and Norma Ray looked unsure of what to say.

"Um… um," Norma Ray said.

Urleen grimaced. "Well, um, we've got some gnomes."

I shook my head in disgust. "Malene, it's one thing for you to lie to me. It's quite another for you to drag your friends into it."

"Oh, she didn't drag them," Lady tattled. "They came willingly. They wanted to mess up Gilbert's display."

I crossed my arms. "Is that right?"

Malene gave Lady a dirty look. "I never should have offered to sit her tonight."

"Then I'll take her back."

"No," Malene said quickly. "I like her company."

"Okay. This has gone far enough. Y'all, let's pick up all these naked gnomes and get them out of here. If you insist on putting all of these up on Gilbert's roof, I will go directly to Tuney Sluggs and tell him what you've done. Now, it's time for everyone to git."

Malene grabbed a gnome. "Leave it to my granddaughter to mess up my plans. I had it all worked out."

"Yeah, and you would've gotten away with it if it hadn't been for some meddling kids, huh," I said, referencing a line from Scooby-Doo.

"That's right," she snipped. "Come on, ladies. Let's get these gone."

"Perhaps," Rufus offered, "I can help deal with some of this mess by removing it magically."

"That would be amazing." I picked up a gnome who was in the act of peeing and nearly vomited. "I think we can use all the help we can get."

Rufus rubbed his hands together. "Ladies, can each of you please grab a gnome? I'll whisk you back to Malene's, where we can dispose of this mess, and then Urleen and Norma Ray, I'll return you to your vehicle."

Norma Ray gave Rufus a toothy grin. "That would be wonderful. My legs hurt from climbing the ladder that Malene made us use. She doesn't know that my arthritis is killing me right now."

Urleen handed Norma Ray a gnome. "I've told you a thousand times, the more you work the joints, the more they lubricate themselves. You have to exercise them, Norma Ray."

"I exercise every day when I make my coffee. I do squats."

"I don't think bending over to reach your stash of orange rolls is considered exercise."

"I'll stay behind and make sure we got all the gnomes," I told Rufus.

He smiled. "Be right back."

In a flash of magic they disappeared. I searched the roof and found that they had, indeed, forgotten a couple of gnomes. I hoisted one under each arm and prepared to climb down the ladder.

That was when I heard a voice coming from below. "Well, Clementine Cooke, sure does look like you're trespassing."

My blood froze in my veins. I glanced down and saw Gilbert Wilcox. He flashed a light into my eyes.

"Don't move. Tuney Sluggs is on his way."

I gulped. Great. What sort of trouble had Malene gotten me into now?

CHAPTER 6

"This is all a big misunderstanding," I said when Sluggs arrived in his bathrobe and cowboy boots. Sluggs was old as dirt and about as bright as it, too.

I stood with him and Gilbert on the front lawn. No, I hadn't even attempted to use magic to vanish after Gilbert caught me. That would have been the sane thing to do. Throw a forgetful spell on his booty and then disappear into thin air. That's what a smart witch would have done.

Well apparently I was not a smart witch. If I was a clever one, I would have done all those things, but instead I heaved myself right down that ladder and waited for Tuney to show up.

Also, I did not actually know how to vanish myself or make Gilbert forget. I lacked those skills. Now if Rufus had been here, he would have been able to conjure up the spells I needed. Heck, he probably had them tucked away in his pocket. But not me. I had not studied in the mystical arts as he had. I was simply a renovation expert who happened to be a witch. It was not the other way around.

"Listen," I said to Gilbert and Sluggs, "I was up on the roof because I thought that I saw some suspicious activity. I was trying to stop someone from doing"—I showed them the naked gnome—"whatever they were going to do with this."

Tuney's bushy eyebrows lifted in suspicion. "And where is said person who was holding this indecent tiny man?"

My eyes narrowed. Did he actually just call a gnome an indecent tiny man? I shot a look to Gilbert, who was also staring at Sluggs. Had Sluggs never seen a gnome? There was a contest that was about to go on, after all. Did he live under a rock?

Well, he certainly dressed like he did.

Sluggs glanced at his watch impatiently, as if he had a hot date with some Geritol.

But in answer to his question, I replied, "I don't know where they went. I saw them, and by the time I got up to the roof, the perpetrators" —it's always good to use big words—"were gone."

"Likely story," Gilbert sneered. "This woman was standing with her grandmother, Malene Fredericks, when Malene accused me of being a liar." He shook a meaty finger at me. The floodlights of his front yard (which were now on) highlighted it to perfection. "Now if I know Malene, and I'm pretty sure that I do, she's behind all of this. She probably sent Clementine here to my house in order to sabotage it with this grotesque gnome." He placed the back of his hand over his forehead dramatically. "Everyone knows that I would never, not in a million years, have naked gnomes in my yard. They're revolting. This is Malene's work. You mark my words, she's behind this entire episode."

I couldn't let Gilbert pin this on my grandmother. Yes, Malene was guilty as all get-out, but she wasn't here, and I couldn't throw her under the bus. That would just be wrong. I'd never forgive myself. "Look, I know that this sounds crazy. I know what I'm telling you sounds impossible to believe. But I did see someone atop that roof, and no, it wasn't my grandmother. I don't know who it was, but they left these gnomes. I was able to run them off. I'm sure they won't be back—ever again. And besides, when's the judging?"

"Tomorrow," Gilbert said through clenched teeth. He shifted his weight on his hip in a manner that I would describe as sassy. "Chief, I caught her red-handed on my property. You'd better do something about this if you want me to back you for reelection."

Sluggs's watery old man eyes bulged. "Well, well. Let's not jump to conclusions. Miss Cooke doesn't actually have any of your property in her possession, does she?"

A flush crawled up Gilbert's neck. "What's that got to do with anything? My law office has always supported you. We've always said that you're the man who will keep our town safe. She is holding a suspicious gnome. Isn't that enough of a reason to take her down to the station? I want to press charges against her for trespassing."

The blood pooled at my feet. Maybe I did need to give up my grandmother. But then we'd all be hauled to jail.

I shot a pleading look to Sluggs, who for once appeared to be on my side. "Look, Gilbert, it's late and I'm sure Miss Cooke is sorry for being up on your roof. But there's no evidence that she didn't see someone up there, and she's holding two tiny naked men." To me he said, "Are there more tiny naked men up there?"

I shook my head. "No. This is it."

"See? I say we call it a night."

But Gilbert's cheeks bulged like he was playing a bugle. "This is outrageous." He thrust a finger into Sluggs's face. "Either you do something about this, Sluggs, or else."

"Gentlemen, I see you've found my sweetheart." Rufus's voice pierced the night. I exhaled audibly as the three of us turned in his direction. "Ah, there you are." Rufus wrapped his arm around my shoulder. I nearly fell on top of him in gratitude.

My, but was he a sight for sore eyes…and arms, and feet. Speaking of, my feet were really burning and tired from having climbed up that ladder and now standing in the front yard. The sandals I wore were not made for all this up and down.

Rufus gave me a warm smile, and all I wanted to do was melt against his chest. "Might I ask what's going on? Clementine, you said that you were going for a walk. That was thirty minutes ago. What happened?"

"Yes," I said slowly, catching on to Rufus's story. "Well, I saw someone suspicious on Gilbert's roof. I yelled at him or her—I couldn't tell which they were—and they disappeared, apparently climbing down a ladder. They left two tiny naked men in their place."

His brows arched with fake interest. "How very…considerate of them."

That lit a fire in Gilbert's craw. "It was not considerate of them at all. I don't believe that Clementine is telling the truth. I believe that she's lying—through her teeth, in fact. I think that her grandmother coerced her into putting those hideous gnomes on my roof in order to ruin my chances of winning the contest."

Rufus's eyes darkened in warning. He did not like Mr. Wilcox being so rude to me. That made me proud. "So that you know—Clementine is one of the most upstanding citizens in this town. She cares for Peach-wood very much. She also has steel-lined morals. She would never, not even for her grandmother, do such a thing as sabotage your chances."

Gilbert lifted his nose in the air and snorted. "The evidence appears to speak for itself. She was on my property. Sluggs, I demand you arrest this woman."

Sluggs glanced at his watch. "Aw, Gilbert, can't we just call it a night? Clementine isn't a criminal."

"She is to me."

"Perhaps, gentlemen," Rufus said gently, "we can come to an agreement, something that will make all sides happy. Now, I know that Clementine should not be arrested. I understand you're concerned for…"

"The sanctity of my yard," Gilbert said dramatically.

It took everything I had not to burst into laughter.

"All right, then," Rufus said without even breaking into a smile. "You want to keep your yard space safe. And Clementine, what do you want?"

"Not to be booked as a criminal, since I'm not."

Gilbert scoffed. I really did not like him. Now all I wanted to do was to wait until he was asleep and pepper his yard with indecent gnomes. I might even throw in some reindeer to really mess with his head.

Rufus rubbed his hands together. "How about this? To make sure that Clementine doesn't have a chance to ruin your yard—when's the judging?"

"Tomorrow," we all answered.

"How about this—Clementine goes with the judges and follows them as they make their way through town?"

Gilbert started to object, but Rufus raised a hand to silence him. "If she's with the judges, Clementine won't have a chance to ruin your yard. She'll be escorted through town, safeguarded, if you will."

"And what about tonight?" Gilbert asked. "How can I be sure that she won't return and sully the sacred ground that I've created?"

I rolled my eyes. *Give me a break.*

"Well, I suppose that you'll just have to trust that this little interaction with you and the police have scared her enough that she won't return—if in fact she was doing anything illegal to begin with," Rufus added quickly, catching the scathing look that I was giving him at the mention that I was being scared straight from dealing with Sluggs. "What do you say?"

Sluggs yawned. Oh, so that was why he kept staring at his watch. It was past his bedtime. "I think it's a good plan."

"Of course you think so. You just want to put your head on a pillow," Gilbert said. "If any of this goes wrong, Tuney, my office won't back you. Remember that."

Sluggs nodded. "I'll remember. I'm sure you won't let me forget."

Gilbert glared at me. "Even though I know you're guilty as sin, I'll go along with this. But if you so much as breathe on my grass, I will press charges against you. I don't trust you or your weaselly grandmother."

That made two of us. There, Gilbert and I were in agreement. "I swear that I have no interest in messing up your chances in the contest."

"We'll see," he said, beady eyes narrowed. "Now, if that's all, I will take my leave."

Without so much as a good night, Gilbert turned and sashayed to his front door, opened it and slammed it shut.

Sluggs tipped his hat. "Y'all have a good night. And Clem, try to stay out of trouble. Most of the time I think you're behind stuff, but this time I actually don't believe it."

"Oh," was all I could think to say.

"Just be careful how much you cover up for Malene. At some point your grandmother could get you into real trouble."

Before I could even think of a way to deny Sluggs's more than accurate claim about my grandmother's doings, he had turned away from us and was strolling slowly to his patrol car.

He got in and left, leaving Rufus and me alone. I gave him a teasing look. "Took you long enough. If you'd dallied any longer, I would've been hauled into the station."

He grimaced. "You wouldn't believe the time I had calming down your grandmother and trying to get those gnomes from her. Of course I didn't believe that she wouldn't return on her own and put them back."

I bit back a giggle. "So you made her give them to you."

"I had to pry them from her hands."

Then I did laugh. "She is something else."

"That she is." Rufus slid a hand over my shoulders. "Come on. I do believe we have a date to finish up."

A zinger of desire snaked all the way to my toes. Thank goodness. The meteor shower was long gone, but that didn't mean this night was a complete disaster. I hooked my hand around Rufus's waist. "Yes, let's finish our date."

CHAPTER 7

We returned to the house and went back on top of the roof to find that indeed, the meteor shower was over. *Thanks for ruining my meteor shower, Grandma.* I had a right mind to call and chew her out for almost getting me arrested and for also squashing a truly intimate moment with Rufus. But if I played my cards right, this night wouldn't be over yet—not for a while, at least.

We took the blanket and spoiled food back into the house. Rufus helped me clean up, throwing away the rest of the chicken. Y'all, it sat up there, exposed to the bugs and what-not, for a good hour. There was no way in Hades that I would be wrapping my lips around another one of those legs.

"I'm sorry about the chicken," I said as I plunged my hands in hot, sudsy water to clean the plates and silverware. "You can blame Malene."

"I don't think it's a total loss." He came up behind me and slid his hands over my arms, running his fingers all the way to mine. I hitched a breath. Actually I just about wheezed and coughed, he'd taken me so much by surprise. His mouth brushed my ear, and my head nearly exploded. "After all, I get to spend a few extra minutes with you."

Minutes? I was thinking more like hours. "You're welcome to help me with the dishes as much as you want."

He did. Rufus's hands covered mine as we worked in unison. He shifted forward until there was no space between my spine and his abs. His breath tickled my ear, and I swear that every nerve ending I had in my body screamed with want.

We washed a plate, and his hands worked over my arms, dripping water and suds all over them. I moaned. Y'all, it was the sexiest moment I'd ever experienced with a man.

I did not want it to end.

His lips found my ear, and he nibbled the lobe. I closed my eyes as my stomach seized. I heard him dry his hands on a towel and then felt the heat of his palms against my shoulders and running down my biceps.

He pressed his hands gently to my arms and slowly spun me around. Our lips met, and everything melted away. It was only him and me. The world could literally have been burning up all around me and I wouldn't have cared even a teensy bit.

This was what I had wanted.

Our lips parted for half a second, and Rufus murmured, "Clementine."

I shivered. The sound of my name on his lips sent me reeling. "Yes?"

He spoke between kisses. "You. Have. Wrecked. Me."

I wound my fingers behind his neck. "Good. How about *you* wreck *me*? In the bedroom."

He stiffened and slowly pulled away, working his hands around mine and untangling them. What? Had I said the wrong thing?

He stepped back. A wall flew up between us, one that I hadn't even known to look for. "I said the wrong thing, didn't I? Listen, just forget I said it, and we can go back to where we left off." I smiled brightly. "Just don't mind me."

He sighed and took my hands, staring down at them instead of up at me. Uh-oh. Was he about to break up with me? No way. No how. All signs pointed to the bedroom, not the breakup room. Not that there was one of those. But you know what I mean.

"Clementine"—his gaze lifted to mine, and the worry in his eyes made my heart splinter—"there's nothing that I want more than to take you into that bedroom. Trust me. I would like that probably more than you."

"Impossible," I joked.

He chuckled. "No, it's true. But, as strange as it may sound, I'd like to wait."

"Wait?" I wrapped my head around the word. It seemed awfully foreign and didn't even sound right. "Wait? For what?"

"For when the time is right."

"I think it's right now." I tugged his arm forward, but he didn't budge. That man was a slab of rock. "Let me show you."

He shook his head sadly. "No. I've certainly not been a gentleman my whole life. In fact, I've been quite the opposite. But with this, I don't want to screw it up. Clementine Cooke, if you'll have it, I would like to wait before we take things to the next level, as you say."

I studied him, and then it hit me. Rufus wanted to wait until things got serious between us—until there was no going back. He wanted to wait for things to get hot and heavy until what? He put a ring on it?

Was this right? Was this the Rufus I knew? Had he been kidnapped? Brainwashed? Had someone stolen him in the night and replaced him with a clone? Had there been an invasion of body snatchers and no one had bothered to tell me?

No way. If Lady had even gotten one whiff of a body snatcher, she would have been screaming it from the rooftops.

"I know you'll think me old-fashioned," Rufus said. So yep, that was it—Rufus wanted to wait to see where our relationship went. If we wound up walking down the aisle, then we'd go farther.

Which had me thinking. "It's because I'm me, isn't it? You think by doing this, that you're protecting me."

He hesitated. So I was right. "I think that I'd feel more comfortable if we waited."

I folded my arms and scowled something fierce. "I'm a big girl, you know. I can protect myself. I know that you once kidnapped me and tried to play Dr. Frankenstein on my powers. I have overcome it. I love you. You love me. I don't see the problem."

He sighed. "You will thank me for this. I promise you. One day, you'll see that what I've done is the right thing."

"Well that isn't today."

His shoulders sagged. "I know this is hard to understand, but I'm doing this for you. I want the choices that we make to be right, and I want to do them together. I also don't see what the problem is with waiting. All we're doing is making sure that when the time is right, it's an even better moment than now."

I didn't say anything. Rufus's gaze searched my eyes, and I responded by giving him a cold glance. Was it immature of me? Absolutely. But it was how I felt at the moment, and all I could think of was how disappointed I was.

"Besides," he added, seeming to either ignore or not notice my chilly stare, "what's wrong being with a man who wants to protect you and who, at the end of the day, wants to be old-fashioned?"

"When I think old-fashioned, I think of banana splits," I told him. "You know, traditional—with the banana on the bottom and all the other good stuff on top. Our relationship is not a banana split."

"No, and you taste much better."

I hated him right then. I wanted to claw my eyes out in frustration or at least scream. I had sent Lady away, for goodness' sake, all so that I could have some alone time with my man. But it turned out that my man didn't want to have any alone time with me.

This was a catastrophe.

He opened his arms for me to walk into a hug. I shook my head. I didn't want his hugs.

Rufus dropped his arms. "I'm sorry if this is a disappointment."

"Disappointment? This isn't a disappointment."

"Oh, good—"

"It's a slap in the face. We were having fun. I thought that our relationship was going to reach new heights tonight. I sent my dog away so that she wouldn't have to hear my moans. But now you're telling me that you don't want to do anything. You just want to kiss some and maybe walk up behind me and do things with your soapy hands that are very innuendo-ish, if I do say so myself."

"I'm so—"

I lifted my hand. "I do not want to hear your apologies. You are old-fashioned. That's what you're telling me. But I think you're also saying that if I was anyone else, you would have jumped into the sack with me. Is that right? But I'm not. I'm me, and therefore I need kid gloves. I'm so delicate and fragile that you won't even take me to the bedroom and have your way with me. Well that's fine. If you don't want to get to know this"—I grazed my hands up and down my body—"then this doesn't want to get to know you, either."

Fear blazed in his eyes. Good. Rufus needed to know what he was missing. And he was missing out on a whole lot, let me reassure you.

"You're misunderstanding," he said.

"Oh no, I'm not." I folded my arms and glowered. "You said that you were old-fashioned. You said that you wanted to see where this relationship was headed. Well, not exactly. What was it you said? You wanted to wait until we reached the next level. What's the next level, Rufus? I'm not moving in with anybody. So that can't be it. So what exactly are you saying?"

He hesitated. "I'm saying that I wanted to make sure that when the time is right, we're both ready."

"Look at me. I'm ready. I've been ready. I was ready when we were eating chicken. I was ready this morning, last night. You know what I think?" I jabbed a finger into his chest. "I don't think you're ready."

Fire danced in his eyes. I was pushing my luck. He was getting angry. Let him. He needed to be angry. Then maybe he'd see how ridiculous his plan was.

"You're trying to bait me," he replied.

"No, I'm not." Yes, I was. But he didn't need to know that. "I just think there's more that you're not telling me. I've never known a guy who wasn't ready."

"Then you've never met me," he snapped. "Don't you think all I want to do is follow you into your room? That's all I want. This is taking a lot of discipline."

"Oh, I bet," I said sarcastically.

"Don't believe me. That's fine. Do what you want. I'm not doing this because I don't care about you. I'm doing it for quite the opposite reason—because I care too much. If something were to happen, I wouldn't want you to get hurt."

I slapped my thigh in frustration. "What's going to happen? You going to walk out on me? We're not married. You can do whatever you want. So can I. I'm a big girl. I think I can handle whatever it is that's coming for me."

He raked his fingers through his hair. "You don't understand. Fine. *I don't want to.* How's that for honesty?"

It was a little too honest, in fact. His words speared my heart and shook me up. "You don't want to?"

"No. I was trying to be gentle, but I see that's not going to work because you're too bullheaded."

I shrugged. It was nothing to be embarrassed about.

Rufus continued. "I want to wait because of how I feel about you. Because I feel that you're special. There. That's it. I've said it. You're special and the last thing that I want to do is sully this relationship."

Huh. I guess he was being rather romantic with a large dose of gentleman on the side. And here I was, acting like a five-year-old, throwing a hissy fit for not getting my way.

When I didn't say anything, he went on. "But I can see that my concern is not well-received. Perhaps it's time we said good night."

He turned and walked toward the door. I found myself stuck to the tile in the kitchen, and it was only when I heard the door opening that I managed to peel myself from the floor and head over to him.

"I'm sorry," I said a bit petulantly.

Rufus glanced over his shoulder. "I didn't want to fight."

"Me neither. I just wanted to have my way."

He laughed and pivoted to face me. He pulled me into a kiss and wrapped his arms around my waist. "Let's not fight. If my wishes are too much, that's okay. I can accept that."

I quirked a brow. "And what? Change your mind?"

"No, not that. But if they don't work for you and you need to move on, I understand."

"Move on?" He meant dump him. What? How did we get all the way there? We'd started in the kitchen, and now I was breaking up with him? Hardly. "No, that's off the table."

"Good." He kissed the tip of my nose. "See you tomorrow?"

I beamed. "Sounds perfect."

CHAPTER 8

I was able to get to sleep that night even though I did it alone and was used to snuggling with Lady. She was a really good snuggler, y'all.

It would have been nice to wake up and cook some breakfast for Rufus or let him cook breakfast for me. I would have accepted either version of events, if truth be told. But having the kitchen all to myself for a few minutes was pleasant, too. After all, today was a big day.

I got to go out with the judges and openly serve my sentence for being in the wrong place at the wrong time.

Which reminded me—I had a bone to pick with Malene.

After a cup of coffee with a heavy dose of chocolate syrup in it, I headed over to my grandmother's house.

She must've had some sort of sixth sense that I was ticked, because she appeared at her front door holding a chocolate-flavored coffee cake dusted with powdered sugar.

Steam curled up from the top of it, and the scents of chocolate and cinnamon trickled up my nose. How could I be royally ticked with this thing before me?

I tapped my foot impatiently. "You know what happened last night?"

Malene rubbed the back of her neck. "I saw it through my binoculars. I can see Gilbert's front yard if I peer just right through the trees."

"So you know that I was almost arrested."

"It did occur to me that might have been the case."

I pointed my finger for emphasis. "What you probably don't know is that I now have to prove that I'm a decent citizen. Thanks to you, I'm going on the parade of gnomes with the judges. Which means that all of them will end up knowing that I was found on top of Gilbert Wilcox's house holding two tiny naked men."

Malene shot me a toothy grin. "Coffee cake?"

"About time you offered." I swept past her into the house. "And where's my dog?"

"I'm here, Clem." Lady padded up to me with a slice of bacon sticking out of her mouth. "Malene's a great cook."

I whipped my head over my shoulder and scowled at Malene. "Bacon? Really?"

She shuffled past me. "They sell Beggin' Strips in the grocery store. Can't be much difference."

"I'm sure there is a big difference." The inside of Malene's house was thick with the scent of the coffee cake. My stomach immediately growled. Malene glanced over her shoulder and smirked. "Okay," I admitted. "You got me. I need the coffee cake."

She sat at her kitchen table and sliced into it. "I knew you'd be here any minute."

I scooted back a chair and sat. "So you thought you'd butter me up. Is that it?"

"No," she said with a sparkle in her eye. "I wanted to add the cherry on top of your date last night."

"Oh, that. Well, let's just say things didn't go as planned."

A sliver of bacon fell from Lady's mouth onto the floor. "You mean I could have stayed at the house?"

"Yes, but then you wouldn't be eating bacon," I pointed out.

"Then I'm glad I was here."

Malene pushed a plate in front of me. "I'm sorry things didn't go as planned."

"It's fine. They went *fine*. We've got a deep, meaningful relationship full of mutual respect and love."

Malene cackled. "Sounds like a load of crap if you ask me."

"I didn't." I cut the edge of my fork into the cake and took a bite. The sponge melted on my tongue, releasing sugar, spices and everything nice. "Wow, Malene. I may have to eat here every day to get my fix of this. Is it a new recipe?"

"Just one I've been experimenting with," she said proudly. "I think I finally got the right combination of cocoa powder and cinnamon."

"I would have to agree." I shoved another piece in my mouth. "And this is the exact fuel I'm going to need to get through my morning. Which, thanks to you, should be a really fun way of humiliating myself."

Malene shot me an apologetic look. "I'm sorry that I got you in trouble."

"You almost got me arrested."

"Everyone knows that Tuney Sluggs was out past his bedtime. There was no way he was going to haul you down to the station. But"—her voice filled with mischief—"think of it this way: now you'll have a front-row seat to all the activities. You'll be one of the first to know who wins the golden gnome."

"As if that's one of my top goals in life."

Her expression soured. "Don't be difficult. You'll have an interesting morning. That's for sure."

Malene watched me with a spark in her eyes. She wanted me to ask her more, dig into what it was, exactly, that she *wasn't* saying. Even though I was annoyed with her, it wouldn't do in the least for me to walk into a bunch of judges unaware, so I sighed.

"Okay, dish it. I know you want to."

She rubbed her hands with glee. My grandmother got way too excited when it came to gossip. There was no other two bits about it.

"Well, from what I understand, this year's judges are filled with some very interesting folks."

"Like who?"

She leaned over and whispered as if we sat in a crowded restaurant. "Like for one thing, one of Gilbert Wilcox's old employees."

"And this is interesting, why?"

"Because that person is apparently disgruntled."

I scraped crumbs from the plate with my fork. "Doesn't sound like a very good judge for an impartial competition."

"No, it doesn't. But apparently Wallace wasn't disgruntled when she was fired."

"Wallace is a woman?"

Malene shrugged noncommittally. "This is the South. You know we have funny names here."

This was true. "I'm guessing you know why this Wallace is disgruntled."

"I thought you'd never ask." Malene popped the last bite of coffee cake into her mouth and made a little sound of pleasure. "That was excellent, if I do say so myself. But back to Wallace. She worked as a paralegal for Gilbert for years. Started with him when his practice was basically nothing. And you know how he repaid her?"

"How?"

"Fired her and hired a much younger assistant. One that supposedly he had an affair with. Let Wallace go"—she snapped her fingers—"just like that. Didn't even give her severance. She went into work one day, and Gilbert was standing beside her desk. Told her that she'd been great, but there wasn't room in the company for her anymore. Supposedly, as Wallace was walking out the door, she got a good look at her replacement, some young blonde thing with legs up to her eyes."

"Figures," I murmured.

"Yes, it does. But anyway, Wallace did not take too kindly to being fired. At least that's what the rumor mill is."

"Did she do anything about it?"

Malene jabbed her finger on the table. "I think this, being a judge, is her way of getting back at him."

"So you're saying that she's saved up all her anger for this one moment of revenge."

"Exactly," she told me.

Well, this trip with the judges could prove to be interesting after all. Still, I felt sorry immediately for Wallace, and I didn't even know her. Having been fired for no reason other than the fact that your replacement was younger, really stank. It was like being the first wife to a rich husband and getting tossed aside for a younger version of yourself. Either way, it wasn't good. Not at all.

"Well, I thank you for the heads-up," I told Malene.

"Oh, that's not the end of it."

"It's not?"

"No. Want some coffee?" She rose and walked into the kitchen with

Lady at her heels, no doubt waiting for Malene to slip her another strip of bacon. Thankfully Malene did not give my dog any more bad food. "Cream and sugar?"

"Thanks," I said, not having actually said that I would take a cup. But I liked the flavor of coffee and there wasn't too much wrong with having three cups in the morning, was there? "Cream and sugar is great."

Malene returned with the coffee and sat a cup before me before taking her seat. "Wallace isn't the only person who's a judge that's angry at Gilbert. Apparently there's an old three-time golden gnome winner who's one as well."

"And that is?"

"Jackson Briscoe."

"Another man?" What was it with all these men competing in a lawn competition? I thought all that stuff was left up to the ladies. Clearly I was very, very wrong. "What happened there?"

"He accused Gilbert of sabotaging his lawn the last year he competed. That's why he didn't win, Jackson said. Of course Gilbert denied the accusation."

"How'd he sabotage it?"

"All his gnomes were put in the ground, hat down, with their legs sticking up in the air."

I couldn't help but laugh. "That must've been quite the sight."

"It was. Whole town saw it and laughed at Jackson so hard, I thought he was going to up and move. Anyway, that was the last year he ever competed in the golden gnome."

"And they let him be a judge this year?" I asked, surprised, given the obvious dislike between Gilbert and him.

"Well, Gilbert only signed on to compete very late. I think he wanted to keep all of us guessing if he would enter." Malene sniffed. "As if we care."

"You actually do care very much."

"Anyway, by the time Gilbert joined the competition, Jackson was already set to judge, and at that point they couldn't change. Peachwood is stuck with who we're stuck with. Can't do anything about it. And if Gilbert had realized who the judges were, I don't think he would have volunteered to compete like he did." Malene cackled. "Serves him right. That man's got an ego like you wouldn't believe."

Talk about the pot calling the kettle black. If anyone had an ego, it was Malene. I rolled my eyes. "I don't think he's the only one with an inflated head."

Her eyes narrowed. "I know you're not talking about me."

"You're right. I'm not. But continue." She studied me suspiciously while I took a sip of my coffee and smiled. "Please. Go on."

"Well, there's not much more to say, really, other than you're going to be in the middle of a group of judges who have reason to grade Gilbert Wilcox low. If he does get below average marks, he'll cry foul, say that the judges were against him from the start."

"He'd be right, wouldn't he?"

"Yep. But it's just desserts, you ask me."

"Why's that?"

Malene ran the tip of her finger around the rim of her coffee mug. "Because Gilbert Wilcox is a no-good, dirty rotten scoundrel. He's an attorney. Isn't that all you need to know?"

I barked a laugh. "Not really. I don't think all attorneys are bad."

"Then you haven't met enough of them." Before I could respond, she flicked her hand dismissively. "But anyway, I'm sure Gilbert sabotaged Jackson's yard those years ago, and yes, he was scoping out my gnomes the other day. I think this was his plan all along—to enter the contest late, cry foul, and make sure that somehow he gets the golden gnome statue again."

"How would he do that by crying foul?"

"Heck, I don't know. But he's squirrelly. He'd figure out something."

"So you say."

She nodded. "That's right. So I say." My grandmother glanced at a clock on the wall. "I don't know what time you're starting, but it's already close to eight."

"I assume Sluggs will be at my house, ready to escort me to the judges. I'd better be heading back. Thanks for the coffee cake."

She pushed her chair and rose. "Want the recipe?"

I shook my head. "Nah. Then I'd eat it all alone. I rather like it with company. Come on, Lady. Stop sniffing around for more bacon."

I gave Malene a loose hug and scooped my dog into my arms. As I marched across the street, back to my house, all I could think of was, *Hello, judges, here I come.*

CHAPTER 9

"All right, this is your new companion, y'all. Meet Clementine Cooke. She's not a judge, but she will be walking with y'all as you tour the homes that are competing today."

Tuney Sluggs stood at the head of a small group of people—the judges, as it were. There were two men and two women, four in all. Which struck me as weird. Weren't there usually an odd number of judges? But since the judges had score sheets, the number of them might not matter. The winner of the golden gnome was based on points, not votes.

The four judges turned and looked at me curiously. I gave a little finger wave. "Good morning. I'm so grateful to be allowed to go on this walk with y'all. Thank you for having me." They kept watching me and I debated lying and saying that this had always been a dream of mine, but that was way too sappy. Those judges would see through me in an instant. And I couldn't have that, could I? The last thing I needed strangers to know was that I had been caught attempting to vandalize Gilbert Wilcox's yard.

The effect a rumor like that could have on my business would be detrimental. Jobs would start dropping like flies.

A man wearing a brown houndstooth jacket (in July!) and wire-rimmed glasses smiled kindly. "We're happy to have you along. If you have any questions about the judging process, let us know."

"Thank you."

Whew. That went well.

Sluggs eyed me like a criminal, all full of mistrust. "Clementine, be sure to stay with the group."

"Yes, sir."

To the rest of them he said, "Now, y'all go and have a great day of judging."

They thanked him and Sluggs left. The man in the houndstooth jacket spoke. "Why don't we all start by introducing ourselves? I'm Jackson Briscoe, three-time golden gnome winner and head judge."

I smiled meekly. "Clementine Cooke. How do you do?"

"Very well." He adjusted his spectacles and gestured to the right. "Next."

A petite woman wearing a flowing red gingham dress and a pencil speared through the bun in her brown hair spoke next. "Most of y'all know me, but my name is Wallace Smith. This is my first year judging, and I can't help but say how excited I am. Clementine, we are so happy to have you here with us. I just know that you'll be a welcome addition. And even though I barely know what I'm doing, if you have any questions, please don't hesitate to ask."

"Thank you," I replied.

So that was Wallace, the infamous woman who'd been fired by Gilbert. She was as sweet as pie. Like, she was one of those people who you knew never spoke a bad word about anyone, went to church every Sunday, talked about the weather when she wasn't sure what else to talk about. She was a nice person. It was obvious.

Wow. Gilbert was a real jerk.

A woman in a green gardening outfit went next. "I'm Wilma Willoughby, and it has been a dream of mine to judge the golden gnome. Many of y'all know that I've held a Beautification Board Award on my garden for years. So though I may not be an expert in gnomes, I certainly know gardens."

She laughed, gesturing for us all to giggle with her, which we did.

And last but not least, the final man, who'd kept his face ducked behind a newspaper the whole time, finally lifted his head, and I sucked air.

Sykes Laffoon! How had I not noticed him earlier?

Well, that was easy. Sykes was a wizard, and he probably had charmed me in some way not to stare at him.

Sykes opened his mouth, and an easy smile crept across his face. For no apparent reason I shivered. It wasn't that I was afraid of him, but he worked for the wizard mafia—for an unnamed and unknown employer.

Sykes's slow drawl crawled through the air. "Morning, y'all. For those of you who don't know me, I'm Sykes Laffoon, though I'm pretty sure each and every one of y'all have seen me at one time or another."

Wallace's eyes lit up when Sykes glanced her way. I got it. Sykes was handsome with his blond hair and trim physique. But did these people realize that he couldn't be trusted any farther than he could be thrown?

His ice-blue gaze landed on me. "Clementine, it's good to see you again."

"Sykes, I didn't know you had an interest in garden gnomes."

Mischief danced in his eyes. "My interests are varied, Miss Cooke. I will be delighted to tell you about them."

I smiled tightly. "You can do so as we walk."

Jackson cleared his throat. "Everyone, can I have your attention? We have twenty houses that need to be rated this year, so we'd better get a move on. You've all got your score cards. Well, everyone but you, Clementine."

"Odd woman out," I joked. "Don't mind me. I'll just be watching and learning."

"Very well," Jackson said. "Let's get started, shall we?"

The first house we hit was Malene's, of course. Since it was on my street, the judges lined up along the sidewalk and studied her design.

To be honest, not much had changed. There were gnomes everywhere. Most of them seemed to be placed randomly.

"She has some design ideas," Wallace said, leaning over, "that work quite well."

I quirked a brow. "Are you referring to the gnome on the toilet?"

Wallace laughed, her hand brushing my arm in a friendly way. "No, nothing like that. The clusters of gnomes, I mean. They seem to work."

Work? Was Wallace looking at the same thing I was? From my viewpoint, all I saw were a bunch of gnomes in different positions (standing, seated, squatted, waving) sprinkled throughout the yard.

"Well," I said kindly, "Malene will be glad that you think so."

The judges made their marks on the sheets, and we continued, stopping at several houses until we turned the corner and headed toward Gilbert's. I wondered if he was home, if a conflict would arise between him and at least two of the judges.

Malene had been smart enough to stay away from her house, but I wondered if Gilbert would be as wise.

We were partially down the street when Sykes slithered toward me. My stomach knotted in angst. What could he want?

"Clementine Cooke," he purred.

"For some reason, my name sounds quite Satanic when you say it."

Sykes laughed, the sound like smoke over rocks. "I'll take that as a compliment."

"I'm not sure you should," I murmured.

"I'm glad that I have your ear for a moment."

"Why's that?" We stopped at a house just up from Gilbert's, one I hadn't noticed before. To be honest, all these gnome homes were beginning to blend together. How much could you really do with gnomes? Especially when they were naughty and pulled down their drawers?

Sykes made a few marks on his score page before directing his focus back to me. "Well, you know that my partner has a vested interest in all things magical."

"I've heard you mention your partner before. But I didn't realize his interests were so specific."

"Trust me, they are."

"Well I'm glad he keeps himself busy," I said, distracted.

Wallace walked up the tiled path toward the house, trying to get a better look at some of the displays. I wished she'd hurry so that this conversation with Sykes would end soon.

"It seems to me that there's some information floating around about you," Sykes said.

My spine stiffened. Surely he wasn't talking about what happened at Norma Ray's barn. *Please don't let him be talking about that.* "I'm sure whatever information it is, it's wrong."

"I don't think so."

"And what makes you so sure?" I challenged.

Sykes slid his free hand into his pocket. He was dressed richly in a white button-down cinched at the sleeves with silver cuff links. His slacks were perfectly ironed and fit him as if he'd had them made by a bespoke tailor.

"Why don't I tell you what I know, and you tell me if it's true or not?" he asked.

Well that would be easy. All I had to do is tell him that whatever he heard was a lie. End of story. No more questions would be asked, and I would be free from this line of questioning.

"Okay," I agreed, arms crossed. "Tell me what you've heard."

He scrubbed a hand over his cheek. "A little birdie told me that you displayed some very interesting powers a few weeks ago."

"What do you mean when you say, 'interesting'?"

"I mean that you called a lot of magic, more than most people use in a lifetime."

I laughed and slapped my thigh. "That is the funniest thing I've heard in forever. Me? That kind of magic?" I dropped my voice. "Whoever your source is, they are wronger than wrong. They probably told you that so they wouldn't have to pay back some money they borrowed from you. Am I right? I know I'm right. Well, it was nice chatting with you, Sykes."

"You're lying," he said in a low voice. "It's obvious. Clementine Cooke, I know that you used a burst of power. I also know someone who would like to meet you."

Fear hit my spine like an arrow's barb. I would not let Sykes Laffoon know that he had me worried if it killed me. He didn't get the privilege.

We started back down the street. There was another house before Gilbert's, across the road, so we huddled in our little group and made our way over. Who would have thought that so many folks would have entered this competition?

Really. The more I looked, the more I saw gnomes everywhere. And these weren't even people who were competing. These were regular folks (I assume) with regular houses that just happened to have gnomes in their yards like there were hood ornaments on the tops of their vehicles.

Okay, nobody made cars with hood ornaments anymore. But you know what I mean.

I decided not to let Sykes think he had the upper hand. "So someone wants to meet me. Why?"

"I think you know the answer to that."

I shot him a scathing look. "Because I used some power? What do they think, I'll come work for them? Do their bidding? Help them take over the planet?" I scoffed. "I got news for folks—it would take a lot more than little old me to help anybody get ahead when it comes to world domination. I don't have that kind of ability."

Sykes chuckled like I was a fool. "No one's talking about world domination. It's just that your power could have its...uses. You could help people, lots of people."

"People like the wizard mafia? I don't think so."

His hand came down on my shoulder. "Don't dismiss my offer so readily. You don't know when you might need a friend."

"Listen, Sykes, I'm not trying to be rude, but I don't think your offer is my kind of thing. All I want is to live a quiet life, a *normal* life. One here in Peachwood. I want to drive my truck to work, fix houses and come home to my dog. That's all I need. If you and your 'associates' desire more than that, that's on you. You can go and find other folks to help you. But with me, you're barking up the wrong tree."

He smiled tightly. "You don't know how I came to work for the people I did, do you?"

Did I even care? Not really, but I would listen to be polite. After all, if you didn't have anything nice to say, don't say anything at all, right? Well, a lot of folks on social media could use that advice. And since I would be stuck with Sykes beside me for at least a couple more hours, I decided it couldn't hurt to just grin and bear it—hear what he had to say even if I didn't give two licks about it.

I did my best to give him a kind smile. "No, I don't believe I know how you came to work for the people that you do."

His icy eyes filled with intensity. "Sometimes you're born with a bad hand, the wrong end of the stick, as it were. That's what happened to me. I was born to parents who didn't care about me. All they cared about was partying. I was an afterthought. As far as I know, neither of them had any magical abilities. Mine started to show when I hit adolescence. I was called a freak by my parents, told that I was worthless. I believed it."

Sykes's jaw clenched. "One of the worst things a person can do is kill a child's spirit. We're all born a blank slate, given the opportunity to either be filled with love or hate. At that time, I was filled with hate. It was my medicine, the only thing I knew. I started to spend time on the streets away from my parents. Trouble followed as it does. The wrong crowd took me in, and I became a petty criminal. It was easy with the magic. I was now the star, able to break locks to houses, ignite the engine of a car with one touch." Our gazes locked. "Can you imagine what came next?"

"Your luck ran out." We were almost to Gilbert's house. "Is that what happened?"

"Bingo. I was arrested, sent to juvenile detention for the list of crimes that I'd committed. My parents had disowned me by that time, and there was no other family. But one day a man showed up to the halfway house, asked to meet me. I remember he wore a ruby ring on his pinky finger and a black suit with a silver tie, his hair so smooth not one strand was out of place. Never in my life had I met someone so rich, I remember thinking. He told me who he was."

I waited for a name, but Sykes didn't give it. Figured. I'd be stuck in the dark as long as Sykes wanted me to be.

"He explained that my magic wasn't a curse. It was a blessing, but that I'd been led astray. He wanted to help me."

Sounded like a cult leader if you asked me. "How?"

"We started spending time together. He showed me how my gifts could be used to help others."

"If you call riding around in a limousine and lending people money helping, that's quite a stretch of the word."

"To you, it might be. But remember where I came from. I had nothing at that point, and he showed me the world," Sykes said mystically. "I was shown that people could be kind to one another, and that a little bit of power didn't make you a freak. It made you special."

"What you're saying is that if you were me, you'd go meet your boss. You'd help him however you could."

"It would be in your best interest to do so."

His words chilled me to the marrow. "That sounds an awful lot like a threat."

"Not a threat—fact. After all, you don't know what you're missing until you do."

What did that even mean?

The group stopped, and I found myself in front of Gilbert's house. *Finally.*

But my relief was short-lived when Gilbert charged out, screaming, "This contest is rigged!"

I rolled my eyes. Here we went again.

CHAPTER 10

Gilbert Wilcox ran down, arms waving wildly. He still wore his bathrobe, and the tails of the belt flew out behind him as he charged toward us.

"This contest is rigged. I demand new judges," he said as his hands curled into big meaty baby fists. Looked like Gilbert was ready to be throwing a tantrum of epic proportions.

Jackson Briscoe grabbed the lapels of his jacket in a relaxed, confident pose. With his clipboard in hand, he met Gilbert full force. "Gilbert, there will be no change of judges."

"I know at least two of y'all are against me." He folded his arms and glared at the group. "Everyone knows that you, Jackson, think that I ruined your chances of winning the last year that you competed. And you believe so, too. You won't give me good marks. You'll give me horrible marks."

Jackson stiffened. "I assure you, Gilbert, that I can do my job as a judge and be impartial."

"Of course you can't. It's impossible. There's too much bad blood."

"I can separate my personal feelings from my professional ones. Now, if you'll let us get back to doing our jobs, that would be most appreciated."

"I'm not going to let you get back to your jobs," Gilbert roared. "I'm calling Parks and Recreation and getting you and Wallace replaced."

Wallace gasped. It was an awful sound. She sounded more pathetic than a blind kitten mewing for its mother. "Well I've...I've never been kicked off anything in my life. Unless, of course, you count when you fired me, Gilbert."

"See?" Gilbert threw his hands into the air. "None of y'all will be able to grade me fairly. I knew it! I'm making the call."

Jackson smiled tightly. "Gilbert, we've already started. You can't get us fired now."

"Oh, can't I? I most definitely can."

The one good thing about their argument was that it had stopped Sykes from talking. I really, really didn't want to have to hear about how his wizard mafia boss wanted to meet me and hire me to do... whatever it was that he wanted. There was no way, no how that I was about to jump into business with him.

But this was getting out of hand. Gilbert's face was fire red, and Jackson's forehead was the same color. He was trying to keep cool, but Gilbert was throwing a hissy fit to end all hissy fits and he was doing so in front of the entire block.

This did not seem to be lost on Jackson, because he glanced around nervously before seething, "What would you like me to do, Gilbert? Give you all tens? Will that prove that no one is against you in this contest? Is that what you want?"

"That would be a start," Gilbert said snidely.

Jackson glowered. "You know that's not going to happen. Look, you need to calm down."

Gilbert placed his hands on his hips. "Well then, I'm making a phone call and getting every score that y'all have made, thrown out."

The entire time, Wallace was just watching from our group, but as Gilbert's attitude became more and more nasty, her face contorted in anger.

Like, y'all, she seemed to be a really nice woman. But from all outward appearances, that really nice woman was about to blow her top.

"Let me just get my phone," Gilbert said.

That was when Wallace charged at him. She did so, head down, like a bull. "You will not call Parks and Recreation." Wallace ran up the sidewalk, her head leading the way. It connected with Gilbert's belly, sending him spiraling backward. His arms pinwheeled as his back bowed. I swear, for a man so round, he had some skinny arms. Looked more like sticks than arms if you asked me. What made them even stranger were his meaty hands.

As he went clambering back, looking like an extra in a filmed karate fight, Wallace screeched, "You are not getting us thrown off as judges. Jackson and me, we signed up months ago and were vetted by Parks. Just because you decided last minute to enter, you can't hold that on us. This has been a dream of mine, a bucket list moment, and you, Gilbert Wilcox, are not going to ruin it."

Gilbert managed to catch himself before he fell flat on his booty. His jaw fell open as if he couldn't imagine sweet little old Wallace, who he'd clearly raked over the coals, headbutting him. "You have become violent. Never in my experience as a golden gnome contestant has a judge personally attacked me. Until now. That's it. No more Mr. Nice Guy."

If that had been Gilbert's nice guy, I hated to see his mean one. I swear that man was nasty to the core. There wasn't a pleasant bone in his entire body.

Jackson wagged a finger at Wallace. "Apologize to him. Maybe that'll calm him down."

"I am not apologizing to that son of a gun," she spat. Suddenly I didn't know who Wallace was anymore. That sweet little woman who'd introduced herself to me had become a spitfire full of vengeance. "Gilbert, you are just about the nastiest person alive. I wouldn't even sit on you if you were the last toilet on earth."

You could have heard a pin drop. I had no idea how we went from gnomes to toilets, but it was fascinating. I couldn't remember the last time I'd born witness to such outright fighting among adults.

Actually I never had before.

By that time Gilbert's whole body was red with fury—not just his face anymore. He wagged a finger at Wallace. "See? This contest is rigged, as I said. Let me go get my phone."

"What?" Wallace teased in more of a tormenting way than anything else, "Your hussy not in there to bring out the phone to you? The woman who stole my job not waiting on you hand and foot?"

The other three judges gasped at Wallace's outburst—even Sykes. Jackson just rubbed his head as if the whole situation was too far gone to save. I think he was right.

"Listen here, Wallace," Gilbert said, eyes narrowed, "what happened had nothing to do with her. It was all you. You were starting to slip. Your work wasn't as good as it used to be."

"That's a crock of bologna, and you know it," Wallace shouted. "You fired me when I was in my prime." She straightened her back and hoisted up her boobs, as if to prove that they were still as perky as they had been twenty years ago. "I'm *still* in my prime. I was the best paralegal you ever had, and if you weren't the best lawyer in town, I would've hired a different attorney to sue the pants right off your fat butt."

Gilbert sucked air so hard he started to cough. "That's it. This is over. I'm getting the whole lot of y'all replaced."

"No!" Jackson rushed up to him. "Gilbert, this is nothing but a big misunderstanding. Right, Wallace?" he growled.

"A big butt of a misunderstanding," she murmured.

Jackson shot her a look full of fire. "We're all able to do our jobs correctly. We can and will judge you fairly. Why, Gilbert, you haven't even given us a chance to do any judging. We've all just been standing on your lawn while you threatened to have us dismissed."

"It's not a threat. I'm about to do it right now."

He turned to go, but Jackson rushed past him, stopping Gilbert's path to his house. "Let's all calm down. I don't hold any grudges about what happened between us. I have been picked as a judge and plan to be fair and balanced in my marks. There's no reason that the three of us can't agree on that. What do you say?"

Gilbert shifted his weight from one foot to the next. "I can if *she*"— he pointed to Wallace—"can."

"Wallace?" Jackson prodded. "What do you say?"

Wallace inspected her fingernails. "I suppose that I can be as fair as possible."

Jackson's face broke out into a big smile. "See? I knew we could come to an agreement. Now, let's all—"

Gilbert's screen door opened, and a woman with dark ebony hair tumbling over her shoulders appeared. She looked about twenty-one and not a day older. "Gilbie, honey, is everything okay?" She peered into the crowd and caught sight of Wallace. "Isn't that your old paralegal? The one you said had a big butt?"

That was it. Wallace's mouth dropped. In a flash she sprinted up the sidewalk, her legs pumping like an athlete's at the Olympics. The next thing I knew, her purse was hitting Gilbert on the head. "Why you dirty jerk! You said I've got a big butt? I'm going to sue you now for unlawful firing! I'm going to take your law practice and wring every drop of money from it. You're going to regret the day that you fired me, you chicken head!"

Gilbert's hair was indeed coiffed at the top like a rooster's. Wallace's assessment had been apt.

"Stop hitting me!" Gilbert's hands flew to his crown. "Quit hurting me!"

But Wallace wasn't having any of it. "I will not stop hitting you! You deserve every lick you get."

By this time we had an audience. Folks were streaming from their houses to see exactly what was going on in front of Gilbert's Gnomeland, USA lawn.

Jackson, for what it was worth, was actually attempting to soothe the situation. He was doing his best to push both Gilbert and Wallace apart.

I took the opportunity to glance over at Sykes. "Why don't you go help?"

He chuckled as if that was the most foolish thing he had ever heard. "I don't have a dog in this fight. Besides, you ever heard what happens when you get between two canines?"

"You get bit?"

"Exactly. I'm staying right here."

That was when the seductress who had started the mess between Gilbert and Wallace announced that she was going to call the police. Wallace seemed to take that as an opportunity to hit Gilbert even harder.

"Take that, you sucker!"

Jackson was doing his best to snatch the purse from Wallace, but she was moving like Muhammed Ali in the ring. She was flying like a butterfly and stinging like a bee, all right. Gilbert was still hunkered over, trying to protect every hair on top of his head.

He was doing a pretty good job of it, too. The only thing was, that man could not get ahold of her purse to stop Wallace's assault.

Clearly the woman had some pent-up rage aimed straight at him, and who could blame her?

I couldn't, that was for sure.

"Take that! And that!"

Jackson fumed. "Wallace, as head judge, I demand that you stop this behavior right now. If you don't quit, you will be removed."

That seemed to knock some sense in her. But it came at the wrong time. I don't know if Gilbert didn't hear Jackson. He did have his arms over his ears while protecting his head, so that was the most logical explanation.

But right after those words flew from Jackson's mouth, Gilbert pulled one of his hands away and moved like he was going to shoo a fly from buzzing in his face. The problem was, at the same time Jackson stepped toward Gilbert. Wallace stopped slapping her purse at Gilbert's head at the exact same time that his fist collided directly with Jackson's mouth.

Everything moved in slow motion. Wallace's hands flew to her face in fright. Jackson's head snapped up and back. His entire body followed him as he sailed onto the concrete. Gilbert's head lifted, and the horror in his eyes as he realized what he'd done, was evident.

But that did not console Jackson.

As soon as he hit the ground, he was back up with his hands around Gilbert's tubby neck. "Why, I should have killed you when you ruined my chances of winning that golden gnome!"

Gilbert gasped for air and gagged. Jackson didn't seem to care. It was like a wild man had taken over his entire body.

That was, until Tuney Sluggs's siren split the air and his voice blared through the loudspeaker. "Break it up, or I'm gonna book all y'all."

I sighed. *Here we go again.*

CHAPTER 11

Turned out, Tuney Sluggs didn't have to take anyone downtown. Jackson stopped choking Gilbert, but not before saying that he'd wished he'd done that sooner. And Wallace tucked her purse back under her arm.

Gilbert's hussy girlfriend (I only called her that because I didn't actually know her name) only showed her face one more time, and that was to help him inside. I didn't catch if Gilbert was going to press charges against either Jackson or Wallace, but needless to say, a representative from Parks and Recreation appeared at Gilbert's and told everyone to go home for the day. Jackson and Wallace begged for the judging not to be canceled. In fact, they swore that it was an anomaly and that Gilbert had started the entire incident.

Which was true, in fact.

So the rep from Parks agreed that the judges could finish the day. Which was a blessing because even though it had been an eventful morning, I was not looking to tie up two days touring gnome-laden yards.

Because trust me—you've seen one gnome, you've seen them all.

So we continued down the parade of homes, and I have to tell y'all, after seeing all the competition, Gilbert Wilcox really did have the best display. His gnomes were clustered into groups, theme-like. There was thought and substance to his design and it showed.

No wonder Malene was jealous of his talent and abilities. When we'd reached the very last house, I was exhausted, ready to be done with the day. Between Sykes Laffoon and the brawl of the judges and Gilbert, I was spent.

This day had been full of more drama than a beauty pageant. Not that I knew that for fact. Actually I didn't. Perhaps beauty pageants had more drama in them than even the golden gnome contest.

It was probably a draw.

"So I guess that's it," I said hopefully, ready to start the walk back home.

Jackson Briscoe pulled a sheet of paper from his back pocket. "Not so fast. There's one more entrant. Came in late yesterday, just before the close of business."

I groaned inwardly. I did not want to deal with this. Sykes Laffoon shot me a triumphant smile. I'm not sure why he felt triumphant, but it really stuck in my craw.

"Everyone," Jackson said, "here are the new sheets, information about the latest entrant."

He passed out the papers. Wallace took hers. Her hair, which had been carefully pinned at the start of the morning, was now falling in thick strands to her shoulders. "Well, what a surprise." She smiled. "I can't wait to see it."

"Me neither," I grumbled.

We marched down the street, and I quickly realized where we were. The new house wasn't too far from the one I was renovating to flip. Great. That gave me a chance to really inspect the neighborhood, get to know the surrounding roads better.

It was an opportunity, and that was how I saw it.

Sykes took a moment to start a conversation. "Have you had a chance to think about what I told you?"

"That your mafia boss wants to use me for evil? Yeah, and I'm not interested."

He chuckled. "You know, there is such a thing as gray. Not everything in life is black-and-white."

"When it comes to magic and using it, it is. There isn't much to me that I see as gray, thank you very much. And let's face it, I don't know exactly what you do, but I have the feeling that since you say you work for the wizard mafia, it can't be good. There's bound to be illegal activity involved."

He laughed again. "Your definition of illegal and mine are probably very different."

"No." I shook my head. "Usually illegal means only one thing— against the law."

"Sometimes breaking the law is done for the greater good."

I scoffed. "You are not going to change my mind about this. No matter how much you try to get me to see things your way, I'm not. You need to go ahead and accept that."

"It's not me who will have a hard time accepting it."

My jaw dropped. Was he suggesting what I thought he was suggesting? That his boss wouldn't take no for an answer? Well, if that was the case, I definitely wouldn't be interested in whatever he wanted. Folks needed to learn that no meant no and some people couldn't be bullied into doing what others wanted. End of story.

"It looks like we're getting closer to the house," he murmured, changing the topic.

Good. I was tired of talking about his mob boss anyway.

Wallace gasped. "Would you look at that. I don't believe I've ever seen anything like it."

"It's certainly…intriguing," Jackson seconded.

"Nicely done," Sykes commented.

Even Wilma praised the yard that everyone was looking at. Problem was, they were all blocking my view. The four of them stood smack-dab in front of me, and I couldn't peer around them thanks to the fact that they were also blocking the sidewalk.

"So wonderful," Wallace said. "Really a grand statement to gnome decorating."

Now I had to see this. Whoever had created the display must have been a genius. Because honestly, I didn't think it humanly possible for gnomes to be discussed as a grand statement. What kind of statement could they make? That it was better to tinkle in a pond than a toilet?

That wasn't much of one if you asked me. I still couldn't see because Sykes's big head was in my way. Wallace happened to turn and spotted me trying to peer around. She took my hand and pulled me forward.

"Come look. You'll love it."

She dragged me through a gap and positioned me where I had a front-row view of the house.

My jaw fell. The house was indeed amazing. There were all kinds of gnome-themed clusters sprinkled over the lawn. There were a band of what looked like gypsies, for lack of a better word. There were also school gnomes and even gnomes enjoying summer, diving into a small ceramic pool. It was hard to pin my finger on a theme, but if I had to pick one, I would have called the display *gnomes having fun.*

"Isn't it great?" Wallace gushed. "I can't wait to grade it."

It was indeed great. It was absolutely charming. There was just one problem.

It was my house, and I hadn't decorated it.

CHAPTER 12

"Malene, what have you done?"

I stood on her front porch. The tour was finished, finally, and my first act after the judges disbanded was to head straight to Malene's for a good talking-to.

She stood behind her screen door. I could hear Willard in the background. "Who's that? Is it Clem?" His head popped out of the kitchen. "Well, don't just stand there, Clem. Come on in. Malene, let our granddaughter inside, will you?"

I folded my arms. "Yes, why don't you let me do that?"

Malene lifted her nose and sniffed. "I think I might be coming down with a cold. It's probably best you're not around me."

"That's a lie and you know it." I took hold of the screen door's handle. She did, too. I tugged and Malene pulled. We weren't getting anywhere fast. "Would you let go?"

"No."

I looked past her. "Willard, Malene's not letting me in."

He appeared with a kitchen towel tossed over one shoulder. "Malene, what has gotten into you? Let our granddaughter inside, will you?"

"Fine." She released her hold on the handle. "You can come in. But I don't know what you're talking about. I haven't done anything."

I yanked the screen door and Willard smiled, opening his arms for a hug. "Good to see you. Hey, you hungry? I just made some homemade potato salad and was going to fix ham sandwiches to go with it."

"Sure. Thank you."

Before Willard disappeared back into the kitchen, he wagged a finger at Malene. "And you be nice to Clem, okay? I don't want to hear any arguing while I'm gone."

"You won't hear one peep out of me," Malene swore.

I scoffed. Once Willard was gone, I whirled on her. "Why did you do it?"

She shuffled past me and sat on the couch. "I have no idea what you're talking about."

"Okay. Fine. You want to play that way, we can."

"Well, I don't want to play at all, but I'll do what I can."

She could be so infuriating. "Fine. I'll get right to the point."

"I wish you would."

"Do not push me, old woman. I am young and I am strong."

"Huh. Last I noticed, all you had was a smart mouth and a small penchant for using magic."

She had a point. One that I wasn't going to argue. When it came to smart mouths and cut downs, there was nobody better at delivering than Malene.

"Okay. I won't horse around. Why in the world did you go to the new house that I have bought and decorate it with gnomes?"

I waited for her to deny it. It was her main modus operandi, after all, denying what anyone accused her of. If she was wearing red lipstick and I pointed it out, my grandmother would say it wasn't red at all—it was blue or some such nonsense; it was just the way the light was reflecting off the color to make it appear red.

Yes, she was most certainly a handful.

"Oh," she said in realization, "that's what you're talking about."

"What did you think I was talking about?"

"Well, I'm sure that I didn't know."

I clenched and unfurled my fingers in frustration. She could be so frustrating to have a simple conversation with. "Okay. So why'd you do it?"

"Isn't it obvious?"

"Not to me, it isn't. One minute I was on the judging circuit walking around with Sykes Laffoon and company—"

"The mafia guy?"

"That's the one."

"He's very handsome," she commented.

"Last I looked, you already had a man. He's in the kitchen, in fact, about to serve you lunch."

"Doesn't mean I can't look."

I raked my fingers down my face. "Can we please just keep on target? Why did you decorate my lawn?"

"So that you'd win."

"What? I don't want to win a golden gnome."

I really didn't. Apparently being the recipient of that little statue meant that one suddenly had a gigantic target on their back. Next thing I'd know, my house would be vandalized. Or worse, I'd find sawed-up gnome bodies strewn across my yard.

No, thank you. That whole thing was not for me.

"Of course you want to win a golden gnome. Everybody wants to win," she said snidely.

"Well, not me. So what can I do? Can you pull my entry?"

"No, I can't pull your entry." She laughed like it was the silliest question in the world. "The contest has already been judged. The winner will be announced soon."

"What I don't understand is why didn't you just use all the gnomes that you had and put them in your own yard? Wouldn't that have made more sense than tossing them in mine?"

"For your information, I didn't 'toss' anything. Me and the girls worked hard to arrange your display."

"Of course y'all did."

"Of course y'all did what?" Willard asked, entering with a tray piled high with food. He settled it on the coffee table. "What did I miss?" His gaze darted to me. "Or don't I want to know?"

I waved a hand dismissively. "Just that Malene decorated and entered my flip house in the golden gnome contest without my permission."

"Malene," he scolded. "How'd it look? Did it look good? Is our girl going to win?"

"You too?" I said in frustration. "Can't anybody see that this is not good?"

Willard passed out plates with ham sandwiches and potato salad. I grudgingly took mine. "How isn't it good?" he asked.

"She doesn't know," Malene told him. "Clem's just upset that she didn't decorate it herself."

"That's not true. If you'd seen what I saw today, you wouldn't want to have anything to do with the golden gnome—ever."

Malene perked up at that. "What did you see?"

So I told them all about the fight between Jackson, Wallace and Gilbert, and even told them the part about Tuney Sluggs showing up. My grandparents did not react the way I expected. Instead of being horrified, they started laughing.

"Y'all are seriously not right," I said. "What's so funny about folks fighting in the middle of the day?"

"All of it." Malene pulled off her black sunglasses and wiped tears from her cheeks. "I would've paid a pretty penny to see that."

"I had a front-row seat. Trust me. There was nothing fun about it."

"I kinda doubt that," Willard said, holding his side. "But to get back on topic—Malene, I can't believe you decorated our granddaughter's house with gnomes without asking her permission."

Malene's eyes widened in disbelief. "You're the one who told me to do it!"

"You did?" I screeched. He shot me a bashful look full of guilt. "Great. So I'm surrounded on all sides by those who are plotting against me."

"We're only trying to help you win," Malene said. "You deserve it."

"What I deserve is for y'all to clean up that mess of gnomes. You're calling attention to me."

What I didn't say was that I didn't need any more attention, not after the conversation I'd had with Sykes. But it wasn't my way to worry my grandparents. Since Rufus and I had been talking about something along those lines, I would confide in him about what had happened.

"Pretty girl like you could use some attention," Willard boasted. "But if it's a big problem, I don't see why Malene and her friends can't go over there and clean up your yard for you."

"Me? You're the person who had the idea in the first place."

"I'm more management than a regular worker." He finished chewing a bite of potato salad. "Try some, Clem. It's delicious if I do say so myself."

I stabbed my fork into a cube of potato and popped it into my mouth. The vegetable was cooked perfectly, and the mixture of mayonnaise and mustard left a creamy tang on my tongue. "Mmm. This is good. I like the relish in it."

"Thank you."

"The pimientos are my favorite part," Malene added. "You know, even though I'm only a worker, I still have my opinions."

He rolled his eyes. "I never can win with you, woman. Fine. You're upper management. But sometimes management has to get their hands dirty. Like in this situation."

"I'm fine with getting my hands dirty. No big deal." She brushed her fingers over her mouth, scattering bread crumbs to her lap. "After lunch I'll call Norma Ray and Urleen. We'll go over and start cleaning up. But I hope you don't win the contest. Because if you do, everyone'll want to see your yard. If it's all taken down, half the town will be disappointed."

"I'll risk it." I took a bite of sandwich and moaned. "Willard, you do make a great lunch. I need to come back more often."

"Yes, Clem," he said with a smile. "I believe you do."

RUFUS CALLED after lunch but before Malene rounded up her old lady posse and took them to my house. I knew this because there was no way that I was going to trust Malene's word about going to my house and taking down the gnomes. No way. I would supervise this endeavor and make sure that those gnomes came down, down, down—every last one of them.

No, I did not feel bad about not trusting my grandmother. She had proved that she couldn't be trusted. After all, in the past day she'd almost gotten me arrested. What kind of grandmother did that to their grandchild?

A bad one, that's who.

Anyway, back to Rufus. "How'd it go this morning?" he asked.

I sighed. "It was a mess, that's what. A fight broke out, and then Malene decorated my flip house's lawn in gnomes. They're everywhere. It looks like there's been a battle of tiny ceramic people in my yard. I wouldn't be surprised if they came to life at night and started killing each other."

He laughed. "I don't think that's going to happen."

"You never know," I murmured. "Anyway, something unsettling did occur."

"I don't like the sound of that."

"Sykes Laffoon, who was one of the judges, approached me about his boss. Said the boss found out about what I did at the barn and he wants to meet me or something."

Rufus's voice lowered to a growl. "Wants to meet you? Or something else?"

"I don't know. Not sure. He knows about me, and it makes me nervous."

"I'll come over tonight, and we can talk about it. How's that sound?"

It would sound great if he'd stay the entire night, but I knew that wouldn't happen. "It's good. I'll call you when I'm back at the house. Right now I'm about to make sure that Malene and her group of merry geriatrics clean up my yard. I don't trust them to do it unsupervised."

"I'll call you later and check in," Rufus said.

"Perfect."

"Oh, and there's one more thing."

"What's that?" I asked.

"I love you."

I smiled, even though he couldn't see it. "I love you, too."

We hung up, and it was right as I approached Malene's house that a car horn tooted as the vehicle whizzed down the street. The car, apparently, was honking at me because it was about to run me over.

Who goes sixty in a thirty-five-mile-per-hour zone? I stared through the windshield, trying to get a good look at the culprit. The car stopped. A window buzzed down, and a wrinkled arm appeared.

"Hey, Clem," Urleen called from the driver's side.

"Urleen, you almost killed me."

The passenger window hummed as it lowered, and Norma Ray's

voice shot out. "No, she didn't. We saw you a long way off. Urleen just wanted to scare you, that's all."

I clenched my teeth because if I didn't shut my mouth, I would say something wildly inappropriate and these women might end up hating me for the rest of my life.

Y'all, it was not good to be on an old lady's bad side. But before I could say anything, Malene strutted down the path from her house, hit the button on her key fob and unlocked her Miata—which already had the top down, by the way.

"Clem, you coming with me?"

"Do I have a death wish?"

She scowled. "I'll only go ten miles over the speed limit. Unless a cop tries to pull me over, that is. Then it's pedal to the metal."

I rolled my eyes. "Since I want to make sure y'all do what you're supposed to, I guess I'll come."

She flashed me a wide grin. "Great. Get in."

I hoisted my purse higher on my shoulder. "What's the hurry? You got a hot date tonight?"

She winked. "Sure do. Willard's going to rub BENGAY on my legs later. It might lead to other things."

Vomit surged up the back of my throat. "Oh. Great. I don't want to keep you from all that."

"Good." She slid onto the seat and shut the door. "Now climb in. We've got a gnomeland to clean up."

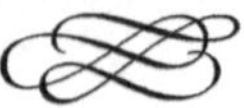

CHAPTER 13

Gnomeland turned out to be a more appropriate term than I had originally thought. My yard did appear to be a smaller, cheaper version of a Disney display at Christmas. It looked like a rival animation company had created a gnome cartoon to do battle against the Seven Dwarfs and thought that by spitting out as many gnomes as they could, they would be able to beat Doc and Grumpy and all the rest in a fistfight.

You know, I might actually pay to see that.

But anyway, of course when we arrived, a crowd had formed around my house. Word had gotten out about the decor, apparently, and people wanted to witness firsthand what all the fuss was about.

At least, I guessed.

"Oh my." Malene killed the engine and pulled up the emergency brake. "How're we supposed to tear down this display with all these people here?"

"Very carefully," I growled.

She eyed me. "You mean to tell me that you're going to rip the joy from their hearts and not even care about it?"

"That is correct. I do not want these gnomes here, thank you very much." I unlocked my seat belt and let it snap back into place. "In a few minutes they won't even remember these gnomes."

She clicked her tongue. "I don't know. They look awfully happy."

Urleen parked behind us, and she and Norma Ray got out and walked up alongside. "Those folks really seem to be enjoying your yard," Norma Ray mused. "Shame we have to rip the fun right out from underneath them."

My gaze dragged from Norma Ray to Malene. "Did y'all pay these people to come out here? Is that why y'all are acting so sympathetic to them?"

"Of course we didn't." Urleen pulled a compact from her purse and fluffed her hair. It was well-known that Urleen carried just about every single thing possible in that bag of hers. If there was something you needed, more than likely Urleen had it. At the moment I didn't need anything, but later on, if I did, I'd ask her for something and prove it to y'all. "But Norma Ray is right. They really look to be enjoying themselves. I hate to take candy from children, and I also hate to snatch happiness from people who love the gnome contest."

I scoffed. "Really? Are y'all really doing this to me right now? We came out here so that y'all could *undo* what y'all had done to begin with. The three of you created a mess in my yard. One that I don't want. You're supposed to fix that."

Malene patted my leg. "I tell you what—why don't we walk up and pretend that we came to see the show?"

"This is not a Christmas display of lights," I reminded her sourly.

"I know that. But if those people are liking what they see, I suggest we let the gnomes stay one more night, at least until the winners are announced tomorrow."

I sighed. Looked like I wasn't going to win. "Fine. But tomorrow it's going down, one way or another."

"Deal." Malene flashed a smile to her partners in crime. "Now. Let's go hear what those people think of our brilliance."

Before I could argue, the three of them had left the vehicle's vicinity and were marching down the street. Talk about a fourth wheel—me, I was the fourth wheel. Those women just upped and abandoned me like I had cooties or something.

I exhaled slowly through clenched teeth and headed on over. Well, if I couldn't beat 'em, I might as well join 'em, I thought as I strolled down the path that led to my house.

Suddenly snippets of conversation filtered into my ears. "So amazing…it's wonderful…one of the best displays in years…bound to beat Gilbert this year."

I liked the sound of that last one. No, I didn't like Gilbert, but I could get on board with besting him and getting my hands on the golden gnome. Not that it was some lifelong dream to win. It wasn't, as y'all know. But after this morning I despised Gilbert and would be happy to see anyone take the prize over him.

I couldn't help but smile as folks meandered through my yard. It also gave me time to appreciate all the trouble that Malene and them had gone to in order to stage the gnomes.

A small cluster of folks stood in a ring near the house. Wondering what all the buzz was about, I made my way over and found them circling a gnome in a glass booth.

There was golden ink scrolling across the bottom in an elaborate design. Written just above that, and right below where the glass ended were the words THE MYSTIC.

"The mystic," I murmured. "What does that mean?"

"Oh," said a woman beside me. "It tells your fortune. This is one of those old-timey fortune boxes. You put in a quarter, and it spits out a card with your future written on it."

Wow. Where had Malene snagged this? "Does it work?"

"Yes." The woman flashed a white card so quickly that I couldn't see what was written on it, but I could tell that something was printed there. "It works. Not sure how accurate it is. You know how these things go. They're just for fun. But it works."

"What's yours say?" I asked, feeling nosy.

"It says that I'll meet a tall, dark stranger." She laughed. "At my age I'll be lucky to meet a short, squatty stranger like one of these gnomes."

She was older, close to sixty, I imagined. "You never know," I encouraged.

"Go on. Get your fortune." She nudged me forward. "Everyone else has gotten theirs."

It was tempting, and the gnome itself was an adorable little pot-bellied guy with red pants, wearing a turban and a gold hoop earring in one ear. It wasn't exactly the most politically correct design, that was for sure. But the gnome mystic had probably been created before people thought about such things.

At least I hoped so.

"This is hogwash." A man waved his paper. "I've never read anything so silly."

"What's it say?" the woman beside me asked.

"Says to be careful or else I'll be in an accident."

The group laughed uncomfortably. "I'm sure it's an exaggeration," the woman said soothingly.

"I've never been in an accident in my entire life. I'm always careful. This whole thing is bologna." He tossed the card on the ground. "Someone else can have that fortune, because mine's a joke. Whose house is this, anyway?"

Nope. I was not about to volunteer that information. The less these folks knew about me, the better. I glanced around as if waiting for someone to fess up, and caught Malene and her crew reorganizing one of the gnomes to face a different direction.

Actually Malene had it facing the street. But Norma Ray kept picking it up and turning it the other way. Then when Norma Ray walked on, Malene readjusted it back in the position she had it to begin with.

Oh, those ladies.

Since no one surprisingly had an answer for who owned the house, the man stalked off, presumably to leave. I took the opportunity to dig in my pocket for a quarter. I found one and slid it into the change slot. The slider gave some resistance, but after a good shove, I got it to slip into the machine and eat the change.

The gnome's eyes lit up a fiery red. Its hands waved up and down as a voice boomed from a speaker. It sounded like its batteries were starting to run out, slow and groaning, but I could understand the words perfectly.

"You seek the wisdom of the mystic. Ask your question. Do not wait too long or else a fortune you will not receive."

Crap. I was supposed to ask a question? I wanted to ask if Rufus and I would ever have our intimate moment, but thought that too silly. After that, nothing else came to mind. Like, nothing. But then I realized this little guy was supposed to tell the future and the most obvious question for me to conjure up would be about that.

"What does the future hold for me?"

The group tittered with laughter. I guess that I wasn't supposed to ask the question aloud.

"Your question has been heard. Your answer is coming," the gnome boomed.

From deep inside the box came the sound of gears whirling. The red lights in his eyes flickered once, twice and then petered out. The gnome's cylinders had died.

"Is that it?" I asked no one in particular.

The older woman pointed down. "There's your fortune."

A slip of paper about the size of a business card had been spat from the machine. I tugged it from the slit. The fortune was hidden between two hard pieces of thick card stock. I started to peel away the cardstock when a loud blare came from behind.

I spun around along with the rest of the crowd. A semitruck came rampaging down the main road, its horn screaming. The man who'd thrown down his fortune stood directly in its path.

"Get out of the way," I shouted.

The man was looking down at his phone, texting someone. The lot of us screamed, and he glanced up to see the semi barreling down.

I thrust out my hand. Magic unfurled from my fingers. Thin strands of gossamer, so faint that if you weren't looking for them, you wouldn't have seen them, jutted toward him. I was acting on instinct and instinct alone. The magic grabbed hold of the man and pulled him to safety just as the semi roared past.

My heart thundered. Its beat resounded in my ears. The man tumbled to the ground with legs visibly shaking. All of us ran over.

"Are you all right?" the woman who'd been standing beside me asked.

"Y-y-yes," he answered. "I don't know what happened. One minute I was just standing there. The next, I was going to die."

"Sounds like you should have paid more attention to that fortune," she said.

He laughed nervously. "That was a close one, wasn't it?"

We helped him to his feet, and he promised to be more careful. Malene, Urleen and Norma Ray, having witnessed the scene, came over.

Malene reached me first. "What happened?"

"That man, he got a fortune from the Mystic, and it told him to be careful or else he'd have an accident." Malene shot the other women pointed looks. "What's that expression for?"

"Nothing," Malene said quickly. "Nothing at all. Could've just been coincidence."

"Seems like an awfully coincidental *coincidence*," I remarked.

"Stranger things have been known to happen," Urleen replied. "It's only a machine."

"Right," Norma Ray added. "One that nearly described a man's grisly demise. What are the odds?"

Malene shot her a scathing look. "Slim to none."

"That's not what—"

Malene clamped a hand over Norma Ray's mouth. "Pay no attention to the old woman in the corner."

They knew more than they were saying, but what did it matter? Tomorrow all the gnomes would be gone—and good riddance to them.

"What's that in your hand?" Urleen asked.

I'd completely forgotten about my fortune. "I asked the Mystic what was in my future."

"And what does it say?" Norma asked. "Puppies and rainbows?"

That woman was not right.

I pulled the paper from its husk. "There's nothing on it. It's blank."

"Turn it over," Malene said impatiently.

I did so. Only one word was inked in black letters across the paper. My throat shriveled to the size of a nut as my gaze skimmed it.

"What's it say?" Norma Ray asked.

I held it so the women could see. "Death," I said hoarsely. "The card says that death is in my future."

CHAPTER 14

"You mean to tell me that little man said that you were gonna die?" Lady asked later when I was back at the house.

I scraped the last of the chicken and broccoli mixture for a casserole into a glass dish and opened the oven door. "Yes, but it doesn't mean anything." I shoved the meal inside and closed the door. "It's nothing to worry about."

"How is it not? Tiny men do not lie." Lady sat on her haunches and stared at me. "You need to march your booty down to that Mystic and hand him back that fortune. Tell him you don't want it."

I laughed. "I don't think it's that simple."

"Simple is as simple does," she replied tartly.

"Um, I think that's stupid is as stupid does. It's from the movie, *Forrest Gump*."

"I don't know anything about a movie. All I know is that saying. My mama used to tell it to me when I was a baby."

"Your mama didn't talk," I reminded her.

"That ain't got nothing to do with it." She crossed to her water dish and took a few laps. "All I'm saying is, maybe if you give back the piece of paper, you won't wind up dead as a doornail."

I chuckled. "It'll be fine."

But it was unnerving reading the paper right after that man had nearly been run over. Malene and her crew hadn't helped, either. They just kept saying it was a fluke, that nothing bad was going to happen.

Then why had my stomach been knotted into a pretzel for the past few hours?

What I needed was a nice meal with a hot guy and maybe some wine. That would make me feel better. Right on cue, the doorbell rang. Perfect. I'd get about forty-five minutes to talk to Rufus, and then we'd eat.

I opened the door to find him holding a small bouquet of flowers. "For you."

I grinned. "Thank you."

He eased closer, pressing the flowers between us. His lips brushed mine, and for a moment they lingered. "I've missed you," he murmured when we parted.

"It's only been a day."

"That's much too long." Rufus brushed a strand of crimson hair from my eyes. "If things were my way, I'd see you every morning, noon and night."

"That sounds like a big commitment."

Rufus chuckled uncomfortably. He glanced at his feet, and I realized that we were just standing in the doorway awkwardly.

"Come in," I told him.

I led him into the kitchen, where I vased the flowers. Lady padded over to Rufus excitedly. "Clem got a fortune that says she's gonna die! You've got to save her, Rufus! Save my mama."

His brow quirked. "What's all this about?"

"It's a long, boring story."

"Try me."

So I spent the next fifteen minutes explaining everything that had happened at the house, being sure not to leave any details out because as soon as I did, Lady added them back in, with flair.

"Remember, that's when you told that man he was being stupid. That he needed to keep hold of his fortune," she embellished.

"That didn't happen."

"It does in my head," she informed me.

I kept on until the story was finished. When it was over, Rufus rubbed his chin. "It does sound a bit coincidental. But it was probably more of a one-off and won't happen again. I wouldn't worry about that."

I poured us each a glass of wine. "You say that as if there is something to worry about."

"Isn't there?" He took the glass I offered. "Sykes Laffoon?"

"Oh, that. Right. I'd nearly forgotten all about that, what with the whole gnome mystic thing."

"We need to talk to him."

"Sykes?"

"Hmm mmm."

"Okay. You want to walk down the street and wait for his limo to pick us up?" I joked. Well, sort of. Sykes did have a habit of showing up in his stretched vehicle when I was downtown. "If we leave now, we might be back by the time the casserole's done."

That piqued his interest. "What kind of casserole?"

"Chicken and broccoli."

"My favorite." He placed a hand over his heart and pretended to melt. "You really do treat me too well."

I straightened the collar of his shirt. "I enjoy it."

We stared at one another, and electricity charged the air.

"What's going on?" Lady asked. "My fur's poking up."

I broke away from Rufus's trance. "Um, nothing."

"Right. If nothing means y'all are giving each other googly eyes, then I guess 'nothing' it is."

"It really is nothing."

"If you say so."

Rufus's face split into a wide smile. "So, should we go?"

"Where y'all going?" Lady asked.

I bent over and patted the silky fur atop her head. "Just to see someone. We'll be back in two shakes of a lamb's tail."

"Do lambs shake their tails?" Her brow furrowed. "I've never met a lamb. I don't rightly know."

"They do indeed shake them," Rufus told her. "And we'll return before you have a chance to miss us."

"What if I already miss y'all?" She lifted her nose in the air and sniffed. "Does that mean you'll stay?"

"I'm afraid not," he answered. "But when I get back, I'm sure that I can conjure up something made of peanut butter for you. How's that?"

A line of drool dripped from her mouth. "That would be fantastic. I can't wait. Okay. Y'all can go. And if I may make one request?"

"What's that?" Rufus asked.

"Make sure whatever it you give me has crunch to it. I need to keep my pearly whites in good shape, and crunch helps me do that."

Rufus smiled. "It would be my honor."

"I don't know nothing about honor. But I know I lot about peanut butter."

I curled my hand around Rufus's bicep. "Come on, or we'll never get back."

"Hold tight." He opened his palms wide. "We might be in for a bumpy ride."

I closed my eyes just before the sound of his hands clapping filled the air. I felt the floor fall away, and knew that we had left my house. Where were we going? I had no idea.

"You can open your eyes now," Rufus said a few seconds later.

I slowly blinked them open. We stood outside a tall wrought-iron fence with rods that were darted at the very top. The gate was open, and Rufus took my hand.

"Come on."

I gazed in wonder at the weeping willows that lined the red brick walkway. "This is where Sykes lives?"

"It is."

The house at the end of the path was a two-story white antebellum with a wraparound porch and matching balcony. The place was huge— like, *huge* huge.

"Where are we? I don't recognize the house."

"We're in Apple Grove."

I quirked a brow. "Never heard of it. Is it nearby?"

"You haven't heard of it because it only appears on the map when Sykes wants it to."

I stopped, forcing Rufus to come to a halt. "I'm sorry. What?"

He glanced at the ground impatiently. "This house, the whole place exists in that town. But like I said, the town itself only bleeps into existence on a map when Sykes allows it. There are times in your life when I'm sure you've heard the name Apple Grove. You've just forgotten because it's enchanted. The whole area is."

"Why?"

He shot me a knowing look. "Why do you think?"

"Mafia?"

"Exactly. It's for protection. If these men do something bad, it's almost impossible to find them unless you've been given access."

"And you have?"

He glanced around nervously. "I did work for them."

"So they trust you," I murmured.

Wow. Rufus had done work for the mafia, but I hadn't realized that their trust of him ran so dang deep. Sykes must've really liked Rufus if he'd brought him to his big, fancy house. Y'all, it was so big. And it was also super fancy. I was only dressed in jeans and a T-shirt. To walk into this place I needed to be decked out in a nice dress and pumps.

Suddenly I wanted to change clothes.

But Rufus did not seem to notice my apparel faux pas. He squeezed my hand and led me to the front door, where he rang the bell.

Darn. There was no turning back now.

And I wanted to turn back. My stomach had a swarm of bees buzzing in it. Sweat slicked my palms, and a knot the size of Kansas had taken root in my throat. I didn't know what to say to Sykes. For all I knew, the only words I'd be able to muster were, *Me like your house. Can me stay here?*

See? I couldn't even form a coherent thought.

But before I could run away to nowhere seeing as how this place didn't even exist on a map, the door swung open and there stood a kid aged about six or so with a mop of brown hair and a sucker in his mouth. Red, sticky sugar stained his cheeks, and bright blue eyes peeked out from under a fringe of bangs.

"Hello," he said.

"Is your father home?" Rufus asked, not skipping a beat.

Sykes had kids? I couldn't even imagine that he had created children with someone. I figured he only existed in his limousine and came out every once in a while to prove that he wasn't permanently attached to the seat.

Before the boy could yell for his father, Sykes appeared. He tousled the boy's hair. "Go on and play."

Sykes's cold gaze swept over us. "I wasn't expecting company."

"Is this a bad time?" Rufus asked.

"Not at all. Just having family over." Sykes, who was dressed in a tropical button-down shirt and shorts, moved out of the way for us to enter. "Come in, please."

As soon as we were inside, the sound of children playing filled my ears and the yeasty smell of bread baking filtered into my nose.

"We don't mean to intrude," Rufus confided.

Sykes shook his head. "It's no intrusion. Meet my family."

I felt about the size of an ant as I walked through Sykes's grand house toward the back, where all the noise was coming from.

We entered what I could only describe as a world-class kitchen, complete with state-of-the-art appliances and slick marble countertops and floors.

A beautiful woman with a thick rope of dark hair stood at the stove. She glanced up at us and smiled. "Are we having guests?"

"No, no," Rufus said.

"Meet my family," Sykes said, ignoring Rufus. "This is my wife. These are her parents and brother and sister, and their children and ours."

The room was filled with about twenty people. Children ran from the kitchen to outside, where I saw a large table had been set up and lights dangled above it. All the women milled about the room, finishing creating side dishes while the men were having beers.

Everyone said hello, and I gave a weak wave. What had we done? I shot Rufus a look that asked as much. We'd barged in on Sykes during his family time. Heck, I thought he was just a creepy wizard mafia guy stereotype. I didn't realize he was an actual person with a family—and a beautiful one at that.

"Please stay," his wife said to us. "There's plenty of food."

"Yes," Sykes said. "We'd love to have you."

"We have dinner—"

"We'd be delighted to stay," Rufus said, cutting me off. "That's very kind of you."

Sykes smiled. "Let me get more chairs."

He left us alone, and I whispered to Rufus, "What changed your mind? And have you forgotten that I have dinner cooking? If it burns, it'll take down my entire house. This ain't good, Rufus. It aint' good at all."

"Breathe." He slid his fingers over mine and squeezed. "Just breathe for a minute."

I inhaled and exhaled hard. "I am breathing."

"I've already worked magic that will turn the oven off. We won't stay more than an hour."

My gaze darted around the kitchen at the women heaving plates outside and to the men, who were arguing about sports. "Promise we'll be gone by then?"

Rufus nodded. "I promise."

Two hours later we were sitting outside under the lights. The dishes had been cleared away. I was as fat as a tick from eating too much food, and we were having the best time.

Sykes's family had been more than hospitable, bringing us into the conversation and telling stories of their friends and other family members that had us in stitches.

The sun had set. The lightning bugs' bellies were flaring, and the sound of cicadas chirping filled the night.

The women cleared the plates. "Let me help," I said.

But Sykes's wife shook her head. "Sit. You are our guest."

The men got up and went inside, leaving Rufus and me alone with Sykes.

Sykes pulled a cigar from a box that he'd magicked and offered one to Rufus, who declined. He cut off one end and lit it. Sykes watched as the leaden smoke curled into the air.

"You're here because of what I told Clementine," he said as a statement to Rufus.

"We are."

Sykes settled back into his chair. "You see all of this—the house, the land?"

Rufus nodded. "I do."

"It all came from work, from being believed in by my boss. From working hard for him."

"I assumed so."

Sykes took a pull from the cigar and let the smoke roll out his mouth. "Clementine could have all this." He turned his focus to me. "A place like this could be yours. All you have to do is sign on with my boss."

I had to admit, I would have killed for a kitchen as nice as Sykes's. Even if I didn't cook in it, I would have loved to have it. It was gorgeous, y'all. But as tempting as it was, I had scruples.

"You and I both know that what your boss wants me to do isn't legal."

"You don't even know what he wants," Sykes said smoothly. "He could want you to create world peace."

I scoffed. "Highly unlikely. I'm not for sale."

"Ah, but is your power?" Sykes leaned forward. "If there's one thing I've learned in my life, it's that everyone has a price."

"Not me." I bristle. "I'm not getting involved in anything that I don't believe in. You said your boss heard about my power. That can only mean he wants to harness it for himself. Like I said, not for sale."

"That's why I came," Rufus explained. "I wanted to let you know that you can use me as much as you want—"

"Rufus," I chastised.

But he ignored me. "I'll do what I can to help. Find more spells, different ones. Whatever he needs—within reason, of course. But leave Clementine alone."

Sykes nodded but didn't say anything for a long moment. Finally he broke the silence. "Come. I'll see you to the door."

And just like that, our evening was over. We said goodbye to everyone, who all gave us hugs, even the kids, and followed Sykes to the front door.

"There's one thing I don't understand," I said as we crossed the threshold. "About this house, I mean."

"What's that?" he asked.

"How are you able to do things like judge the golden gnome if you live in this place?"

Sykes laughed. "Easy. I have two houses. One in Peachwood and one here, where I cannot be touched."

Well, that made sense. "Thank you for your hospitality. And please thank your wife for taking us in at the last minute."

Sykes smiled. "Absolutely."

"I'll bring a gift for her next time," Rufus said.

"No need," Sykes replied.

"Sorry things aren't going to work out with your boss." I nervously dug my toe into the outdoor rug. "But I'm sure he'll understand."

Sykes smirked. "Oh, this isn't over yet."

A fissure of fear snaked through me. "What do you mean?"

"The boss always gets what he wants. Always. You'll come around, Clementine Cooke. You just wait and see."

With that, Sykes shut the door in our faces and we were plunged outside, into the night.

CHAPTER 15

The next day I woke up feeling a bit crappy. After Sykes made his ominous prediction, Rufus and I came back to my house, but to be honest, I wasn't in the mood for any more conversation.

"The boss may get a lot of what he wants, but he's not getting you," Rufus had said.

I thanked and hugged him. Rufus told me again that he would protect me. "I know you will," I had said. "But right now I'm tired and need to rest."

He had given me a hesitant look. I'd nearly said that I needed an extra bed warmer even though it was nearly eighty degrees outside with ninety percent humidity, but I'd kept my mouth shut. Rufus wasn't going to budge on the whole keeping-my-purity thing, and I didn't feel like thinking about it anyway.

So I went to bed and awoke feeling about the same level of blah as I had felt when I went to sleep.

I woke up, made breakfast and decided to head over to my flip house to start tearing down the wall in one of the bedrooms to make room for a master bath suite. Breaking things always made me feel better.

So I headed over with Lady in tow. When I arrived at the house, there was a crowd gathered on my lawn—again.

"What the…?"

"Why're all those people here?" Lady asked.

"I have no idea."

I parked and with my tool belt under one arm and Lady in the other, I headed over to see what all the hubbub was about.

"What's going on?" I asked.

The crowd parted, and the woman I'd met the day before, the older woman, blinked up at me. "Oh, you're back! Did your fortune come true?"

"Huh?" Then I spotted the gnome mystic beside her. Crap. With everything that had happened in the last day, I'd completely forgotten about the gnome and its predictions.

I'd also forgotten about my own fortune, that the word *death* had been written on my card. It was just my luck, wasn't it? Not only did Sykes Laffoon's boss want my power for some unknown reason, but I also had to somehow manage to avoid my own death.

I was not liking this week at all. As far as I was concerned, it could go back into last week and never rear its ugly head.

But the woman was still waiting for an answer, so I murmured, "Nothing's happened yet." And just to be polite I said, "How about you?"

"I met him," she squealed. Yes, the woman actually squealed. "After I left here yesterday, I went to Bender's for a coffee, and standing there was a man I hadn't seen since high school. He'd moved away and gotten married. But his wife passed on about a year ago, and he decided to return to Peachwood." She grabbed my arm like we were soul sisters. "And guess what? He had dark hair and was still tall! He hasn't shrunk like I have."

"You shrank?"

She shrugged. "It comes with age if you don't stretch out your spine good every day. But never mind that. Do you want to know the best part? He asked me out—on a date! We're having dinner tonight. So I came back to see what my next fortune will be."

I frowned. "Since you already had one fortune go so well, why do you need another?"

She glanced right and left, lowering her voice before speaking. "I think this box here doesn't *see* your fortune. I think it *makes* your fortune."

What? "Why would you think that?"

"Because I'm not the only one who returned. See? These were all people from yesterday, too."

In fact, they were. I recognized a few faces, including that of the man who'd nearly been run over by a semitruck. What? Was he cruising for a bruising or something? After the first fortune, I would have left well enough alone.

The man brandished a card. "It says that money's coming my way. Woo-hoo! Money!"

He showed a few spectators the card before turning around to leave. He'd only walked a few steps when he stopped and pointed. "There's twenty dollars!" He bent over and picked up the bill. "My fortune's already come true. Whoever owns that mystic better not get rid of it or else they'll have a bunch of angry people on their hands." He shoved the bill in his pocket. "Money today. What will tomorrow bring?"

The woman grinned at me. "See? I think it makes fortunes."

Well if that gnome made fortunes, then it saw death in my future. Why was it giving other people good outcomes and leaving me in the dust?

As folks clambered around to ask their questions, I stepped in. "Okay, everybody. I know we've all had some fun, but this mystic isn't real. It's just a box and a plastic gnome."

They eyed me as if I was full of lies. I did not particularly like the looks on their faces, but I also did not enjoy having a crowd on my lawn every day. The gnomes had to go and the mystic with them.

"Y'all, this is my property. You can each do one more fortune, but after that, this gnome is going back to where it came from." A collective groan slipped from the crowd. "I'm sorry, but it is. So, do you're thing because it'll be gone within an hour."

With that, I left, heading inside with Lady still tucked under my arm. "Don't you think you were awfully harsh?"

"No, I don't think so at all. I can't keep that mystic here forever. Besides, it's just a bunch of malarky. It's not real."

"They seem to think so."

I had no comment.

Once we got inside, I pulled out my cell phone and called Malene. "What are you doing?" she asked.

"Calling you." I mean, was that a trick question? "I need you to come clean up these gnomes ASAP. That one mystic thing is giving me the creeps. Folks seem to think its fortunes are real."

"Huh. Isn't that interesting?"

"No, it's not interesting. I would like it gone."

"Fine. But before I do that, you need to do something for me."

I nearly exploded. "Malene, this is not one of those situations where you do something for me and I do something for you. Do I have to remind you that you were the person who put the gnomes on my lawn? If anyone is going to be doing anything for anybody, it is you. Not me. Got it?"

Who did my grandmother think she was, anyway? She did not run this conversation or my life. That was not how things went with us. She was supposed to do as I wanted because she had littered my front yard to begin with.

"Don't get your panties in a wad," she snipped. "I'm down here by Bender's. The officials are about to announce the winner of the golden gnome. Gilbert Wilcox is here, too. I just thought that if they mentioned your name, you would like to be here to accept the award."

I groaned. As much as I didn't want to go—and I didn't because the entire contest had caused me nothing but trouble—it wouldn't be a bad idea to head on down. After all, if I did happen to win a trophy, it would look strange if I wasn't there to pick it up. Now wouldn't it?

"Fine. I'll arrive in a minute. But after that, you're coming up here and you're getting rid of these gnomes—all of them. Do you hear me?"

"Yes, Mother," she said sarcastically, "I hear you. I'll call the girls so that they'll be ready. I wouldn't want to keep Your Highness waiting."

"Honestly, you don't have to act like that."

"Like what?" she said innocently.

I shook my head in frustration. "I'll be down in five."

"See you then, chicken."

Do not ask why my grandmother liked to call me *chicken*, but she did. It was very strange. But no stranger than she was, I guessed.

I plucked Lady from the spot on the floor that I'd deposited her on. "We're heading out to hear who won the golden gnome."

She glanced up at me with sad puppy-dog eyes. "Will there be treats?"

I exhaled. "Yes. There will be treats. I'll make sure you get something."

Otherwise I wouldn't hear the end of it.

So, ten minutes and one doggy treat later, I found myself standing downtown, at the corner where Bender's coffee shop was. A small podium and microphone had been set up, and a few folks were milling around. I found Malene immediately. Urleen and Norma Ray were already standing beside her, patiently waiting for me.

"Well, it's about time you showed up," Malene said in a clipped voice.

So much for patiently waiting. "Sorry, I had to stop into Bender's and get Lady a treat. She was hungry."

"You're just lucky they haven't announced the winner yet," Norma Ray added.

"Why's that?"

"Because we can't wait to see the look on Gilbert's face when your name is called," Urleen added.

"That'll show him," Malene said with a cackle. "He'll learn what it's like to lose. He deserves it."

"Who deserves what?"

We turned around to see Gilbert hovering behind us. A smirk was plastered on his face, his expression saying, *Gotcha!*

Yep, he had caught us talking about him, hadn't he? Just my luck.

Malene scowled at him. "You know what you deserve."

Gilbert's beady eyes took me in. "All I know is that a few gnomes and one with supposed mystical abilities aren't going to win anybody a prize. Right, Clementine?"

How did he already know about the mystic? "I have no idea what you're talking about."

"You couldn't destroy my gnomes, so you decided to attempt to outdo me." Gilbert threw back his head and laughed dramatically. "Well, good luck to you on that. I'm the winner in this town. No one is going to best me except for...me!"

What? That made absolutely no sense. Well, someone sure did have an overinflated ego, didn't they?

I patted Gilbert's shoulder. "You just go on and keep thinking that."

He wiggled his brows. "No one's going to give the golden gnome to a person who's causing calamities in town."

I glanced left and right, trying to figure out who he was talking about. "Are you referring to me?"

"Of course. Who else would I be talking about?"

"Well, I really don't know because I'm not causing any calamities."

He pursed his lips and turned away. That had been strange. What had he meant, causing calamities? I wasn't causing any calamities. At least, not that I knew of.

Before I had a chance to ask Gilbert what in the world he was referring to, Jackson Briscoe took a spot on the podium. Tuney Sluggs joined him, I suppose to keep the peace in case some ornery folks got ticked that the wrong person won the golden gnome.

"Here it comes," Malene said.

Norma Ray took my hand. "I'm so excited for you, Clem."

"Y'all, I'm not going to win," I told them.

"You don't know that," Urleen chimed. "This could be your year."

Jackson cleared his throat. "Thanks to all of y'all who've joined us in celebration of the golden gnome contest. I won't keep you long. In fact, I'll make this short and sweet. This year's golden gnome goes to... Clementine Cooke!"

The crowd erupted into applause. I was shocked. Literally shocked. My feet wouldn't move, so Malene shoved me toward the podium. Finally my head realized exactly what had happened. I had won. I had actually done it!

Well, not me. But Malene and her crew had done it.

I took the golden gnome from Jackson Briscoe. "Thank you. Wow. This is heavy."

Jackson shook my hand. A photographer stepped up and shot a few photos, and then I was drenched from head to foot.

Shocked, I glanced over to see Gilbert Wilcox holding an empty cup of water. "I was robbed," he yelled. "Clementine Cooke stole the golden gnome from me!"

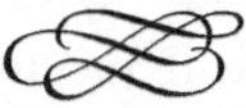

CHAPTER 16

"Gilbert sure didn't like you winning, did he?" Malene handed me a towel. "That really bunched up his boxers."

"Coffee anyone?" Urleen asked, walking over to my pot and starting it without my consent. "I could use a cup."

"Did you bring any cookies?" Norma Ray asked. "Afternoon coffee is always best with cookies."

Urleen opened her purse and pulled out a blue tin. "Will Royal Dansk do?"

Norma Ray nodded eagerly. "They sure will."

Why was I even here? These women didn't need me in order to march into my house and take over my life. I blotted my wet clothes with the towel. "Thanks for coming over."

"It's the least we could do." Malene patted my shoulder. "After Gilbert's childish display, of course you needed support."

Gilbert had doused me with water. Perhaps he thought I would melt like the Wicked Witch of the West. I don't know. But after that had happened and he'd shouted all kinds of horrible things about me (none of which were true, by the way), Tuney Sluggs had tried to calm him down. Then Gilbert turned on Tuney and screamed that he was going to make sure the chief of police never got reelected. Jackson tried to calm the situation, but Gilbert yelled that the contest had been rigged and that Jackson hated him and would do whatever he could to make sure that Gilbert never received another golden gnome.

To be quite honest, after that little display, Gilbert didn't deserve the golden gnome. He deserved a good fanny spanking, if you wanted my opinion.

The gnome itself was adorable. Really, it was. A simple golden statue about eight inches tall. I had already decided it would take a spot of honor and be put on the mantle in my living room. Or maybe the floor. After all, gnomes usually went on the ground.

"Gilbert Wilcox is a jerk," Norma Ray said.

"Yes, but now it's all over." I sighed, relieved at the sentiment. "And we can all go on with our lives. In fact, after we have coffee and cookies, why don't we go down and get rid of the gnomes? That mystic one gives me the creeps."

The trio exchanged a look.

"Yeah, that mystic one is getting a lot of attention," Lady said. "Clem's got people crawling all over her yard like ants. They want one of those little fortunes. Say they come true."

I hoped not. After all, I still had one that promised death. That fortune needed to stay on that piece of paper and never become the future.

Malene rubbed the back of her head nervously. "Is that right?"

"That's right," I said, deflated. "I met a woman who had it foretold that she would meet a man and she did. Another man barely escaped getting squished. His next fortune said he'd come into money. Next thing we knew, he'd found twenty dollars."

Urleen pushed her glasses up her nose. "I'd hardly say that's the same as coming into money."

"But it does seem strangely coincidental," I prodded.

"Yes, I suppose so." She tapped her foot impatiently. "Is that coffee done, yet?"

I peeked over her shoulder. "Just about."

"Well, I tell you, as soon as we find out where that mystic came from, the better off we'll be," Norma Ray said. Then just as quick as those words had left her mouth, she slapped a hand across her lips.

The room suddenly became deathly silent. My gaze darted to all three of the women who were suddenly quite taken with the tile of my kitchen floor.

"What exactly does that mean, once we find out who left the gnome?" I asked.

No one answered.

"Malene," I growled. "You tell me right now what's going on. I thought y'all planted all the gnomes in my yard."

She plucked a napkin from a holder and twisted it between her fingers. "Well, we planted *most* of them."

Alarm bells sounded in my head. "What does that mean, exactly?"

"It means," Norma Ray informed me, "that one of the gnomes appeared out of nowhere."

"The mystic," I whispered, sounding a heck of a lot breathier than I originally intended.

She nodded. "The mystic. One day it wasn't there and the next, it was."

Malene jabbed a finger in the air. "Then you wanted us to clear out the space."

"Which we were happy to do, by the way," Urleen chimed.

"And we would have," my grandmother confirmed. "Remember, you're the one who told us we could stop."

"I'm not going to chastise you."

"Good. Because we're old and we deserve better." Malene sniffed. "But yes, you may have noticed us giving you a strange look when we were over there."

I did indeed remember such a look. The three of them had glanced at me strangely. Now I knew why. "That was because y'all saw the gnome mystic."

"Correct," Malene told me. "We saw him and weren't sure where he had come from."

"We also were worried," Norma Ray said. "We'd heard about such a gnome before."

Anger in the form of heat crawled up my neck. "And y'all didn't tell me? You didn't bother to say anything?"

Malene narrowed her eyes at Norma Ray. "That's because we weren't sure what it was, exactly."

I closed my eyes, pinched the bridge of my nose, and inhaled and exhaled slowly, trying to calm down. It wouldn't do to scream at these women. But screaming was what every bone in my body needed.

I spoke very slowly so that they would understand everything that came out of my mouth. "Let me get this straight. Y'all saw the mystic and had heard of such a thing before, but y'all decided not to tell me."

Urleen took a sip of her coffee. "Let's go back a bit."

"Yes, lets," I said snidely.

Urleen shot me a clipped look. "When we arrived at your house, our plan was to clean up. A crowd was gathered. We paid them little attention because folks always tour the gnome homes. Then we saw the mystic and weren't sure if it was what we thought it was."

"Which is?" I asked.

Urleen pulled off her glasses and set them on the table. She rubbed her eyes for a long moment as if trying to come up with a lie on the fly. It would not have surprised me in the least if that was true.

Finally she spoke. "A long time ago, when I was a girl, there was a man in town who ran a shop of curiosities."

"Curry what?" Lady asked.

"Curiosities," Urleen explained. "That means interesting collectibles."

"Oh, I thought it was food," my dog said.

Of course she did. That was all Lady thought about.

"Not food," Urleen said. "Mr. Wonder had everything, from small pieces of furniture to baubles. If you were looking for something intriguing to buy, that was where you purchased it."

"It does sound intriguing," I said.

"But what we didn't know was that some of the pieces in Mr. Wonder's collection were, how should I put it, of a deviant nature."

"They were cursed," Malene explained. "Just come out and say it."

"Yes," Urleen said. "They were like that. No one knew that at first, of course. I'm not even sure if Wonder knew it."

"If he knew it, why would he have sold the objects?" Norma Ray asked. "That doesn't sound like a very nice thing to do."

"So maybe he didn't realize the truth," Urleen corrected.

"That sounds about right." To me, Norma Ray said, "Mr. Wonder was such a nice man. I always had a hard time believing that he would be devious on purpose."

"I see," I said.

"As I was saying," Urleen interjected. "Most of the objects were completely safe—toys you could take home to children, a new knick-knack for your wife's curio cabinet." Her eyes darkened. "But others were not."

"And let me guess, the mystic gnome is one of them."

"He wasn't in a glass case then," Urleen explained. "He was a fat gnome with the turban on his head, laughter in his eyes. But Old Man Tomlinson bought him, I remember. Planted him smack in his front lawn."

Urleen stopped and an uneasy quiet blanketed the room. Whatever she had to say next, it wasn't going to be good. That much was certain.

"There were little things at first that we heard about—Mrs. Tomlinson left Mr. Tomlinson. Then he planted a vegetable garden in his backyard, and while all the neighbors with beautiful gardens yielded gorgeous tomatoes and waxy cucumbers, Mr. Tomlinson's failed. Everything in it shriveled down to nothing. But that's not the worst of it. Tomlinson's hair started to fall out and so did his teeth. There was no reason for it, no cause—no medical explanation. That's what the doctors said."

I shivered. This story was worse than I had thought it would be. "There was nothing they could find that was the cause?"

"Nothing except for a curse," Urleen explained. "People started to whisper about it. Some said that Tomlinson had been rebuked by God. Others said he had been marked for foul things to happen to him. But no matter what anyone said, the one thing everyone agreed on was that none of the bad had started to happen until he displayed that gnome. People suggested he get rid of it. They told him that if he gave it back to Wonder, then maybe his luck would change."

"And what did Tomlinson say?" I asked.

"By that time people had realized that some of what Wonder sold was bad news. They took objects back to him. Wonder always said that he didn't stock them on purpose. I don't know if that's true. I think he had a knack for attracting what was evil. And then he sold it, innocent or not. But anyway, it all came to a head when Tomlinson's house burned to the ground."

"Oh no," Lady said.

Oh no was right. That poor man had suffered so much and then to lose his house on top of it all? What a terrible blow. "How bad was the damage?"

"He died," Urleen said coldly. "Suffocated in his sleep. Not one thing from the house and the area immediately surrounding it survived except one."

"The gnome," I whispered.

She nodded. "Only that. When people discovered it, they took the gnome and attempted to destroy it. But as you may have guessed, that didn't work. It couldn't be destroyed. It couldn't be cut. It couldn't be burned. It couldn't be melted. Nothing would turn it to dust. So one of the wizards in town said he would take care of it. Everyone thought it had been destroyed. But then—"

"It turned up," I said.

She nodded. "It did. Several years later. Just showed up at the county fair in a box. Those who had seen the thing before recognized it immediately. Oh, it had the turban and was now called a mystic, but they knew the truth. The gnome was evil."

"What happened?"

She shrugged. "People tried to get it taken down. They told the county fair officials that the thing was evil. But no one listened. The next night, a tornado hit the fair. Killed dozens of people. It was later said that every one of those people had gotten a fortune from the mystic."

A pit opened in my stomach. I had gotten a fortune. Granted, mine had been pretty open about my future. Gone were the days of the gnome pussyfooting around, apparently.

"It disappeared again," Urleen said, "until now."

"And it's at my house."

She nodded. "Exactly."

I shot out of my chair. "Why didn't you take it down before now? Why have you let it stay up?"

She shook her head. "You have to understand, my mind has been foggy. I've forgotten some of the stories. These things go way back and deep in the recesses of my memory. It's only now that we're talking about it that I truly remember the history of the gnome."

And my life now depended on Urleen's shoddy memory. I was in trouble.

She pressed her fingers to a wrinkle on her pants, attempting to iron it out. "Now the gnome is back. It's been gone long enough for everyone to forget what had happened—what evil the thing had wreaked in people's lives."

"But I don't understand." I ran my fingers over the rim of my coffee cup in thought. "There are people who have received good fortunes from it, positive outcomes."

She clucked. "Don't be fooled. The fortunes might be good to begin with, but they always turn bad. Always." Her eyes flared as if a thought had just occurred to her. "You haven't received a fortune, have you?"

I nodded, unable to bring myself to speak.

"And what did it say?" Malene prodded, worry laced thick in her voice.

"It said death," I told them in a shaky tone. "It said that there's death in my future."

CHAPTER 17

"Are you sure that we shouldn't even *try* to destroy this thing?" I asked, heaving a shovel over my shoulder. I could do it. I could break the case that the gnome sat in. It would be easier than demolishing a wall, and I had plenty of experience with that.

"The box might break, but the gnome won't," Urleen told me. "No. We'll have to get rid of it another way."

"That stinks," I said.

As soon as the women had discovered what my fortune said, they'd insisted on heading over to my flip house so that we could vanish the gnome. I had wanted to bring along a chainsaw, some weights so that it could be sunk in the darkest depths of a nearby lake and some fireworks to see if it could be launched into space, but the women had talked me out of all those things.

I really didn't understand why, to be honest. All those ideas sounded about a thousand times better than what we were about to do now—which was to make it disappear.

Heck, these old women barely had any magic between them. How exactly were we going to whip up an old-fashioned banishing?

According to Malene, that was the easy part. She had such a spell hidden in her house.

Go figure.

We had waited until nightfall to attempt to work the spell.

"Let me get the magic." Malene pulled a mason jar from her Michael Kors purse (nothing but the best for my grandma) and lifted it so all of us could see.

The orb inside the jar was a deep purple, almost the color of midnight, ringed in a vibrant blue.

"Do you know how to use that?" I asked.

She smirked. "Of course I do. We pull out the orb and squash it between our hands. Then we'll do a little chant."

"A chant?" They usually didn't say anything when using a spell. "Are you sure?"

"Oh, your grandmother has banished lots of things in her life," Norma Ray explained. "From boyfriends to pesky ants that were trying to eat her picnic. She's a pro."

"Norma Ray, I would appreciate it if you didn't tell all my secrets."

My jaw dropped. "You banished a boyfriend?"

Malene hiked a shoulder to her ear. "He wasn't gone very long. Just a little while."

As if that made it better. Remind me not to ever, and I mean ever, get on Malene's bad side. "Okay, well, are we ready?"

Malene nodded. "Ladies, join hands."

We did as she said. When my grandmother was satisfied that we were in fact, all set, she unscrewed the jar's lid. The orb fluttered at the bottom for a moment, but like a trapped insect, it sensed that it was free and started to climb from the jar.

Malene took hold of it in one fist. "*Spell of banishment, spell of darkness, come to us and hark us. We need thy help to banish one made of porcelain and set in the sun.*"

I didn't know about the harking or the gnome "setting" in the sun, but I was all in.

Malene took our hands and gestured for us to repeat the chant. In unison we said, "*Spell of banishment, spell of darkness, come to us and hark us. We need thy help to banish one made of porcelain and set in the sun.*"

The orb streaked around the gnome, making a circle. It moved slowly at first but then picked up speed, whirring faster and faster. Purple and blue magic made a tail of light that streamed behind it. The air buzzed with magic. My hair rose from the electricity filling the air.

The gnome's face lit up, and I swear the evil little creature stared at me as the magic wove. The box became engulfed in a blinding light. A bright flash pierced the air, and I closed my eyes to keep my retinas from burning out. Lord, wouldn't that just be the be-all end-all? If I wound up blind from this stupid mystic gnome?

Well, when I opened my eyes a few seconds later, it did take a second to adjust. But once the light flares receded from the corners of my eyes, I realized that the mystic was gone.

I jumped up and down. "You did it, Malene! You did it!"

She actually took one hand and patted herself on the back. "That was a fine job if I do say so myself."

"You should say so because it was awesome. Thank you so much." I wrapped my arms around her thin frame and gently squeezed her. "I'm so proud of you. I didn't know you had it in you."

"That makes two of us," she mumbled.

"I hope you're kidding."

"I am."

I hugged Urleen and Norma Ray. The four of us exhaled. "Okay," I said, pointing to the rest of my yard. "First thing tomorrow?"

"We'll clean up the rest of it," Malene said. "We promise."

"Thank you." We started to walk away, and a thought occurred to me. "Well, we've gotten rid of the mystic, which is great. But I've got one question. If y'all didn't put it in my front yard, then how'd it get there?"

We stopped in front of Urleen's boat of a car. She spoke. "That's something that is bothering me, too. As much as I hate to say it, there's only one plausible explanation—someone put it there."

I frowned so hard I actually felt a divot form between my eyes. Urleen was right. Someone had placed the gnome in my yard. Someone who probably knew who owned the house—meaning, me.

Or maybe someone didn't know who owned the house, but they had seen the gnomes before the contest started. Maybe that someone was awfully competitive and wanted to win the golden gnome. Correction, *would do anything* to win such a thing.

I wondered who that could have been? Someone who had a real problem with not winning the award? Now, who could that be?

Just kidding, I knew exactly who it was—Gilbert Wilcox.

Well that sucker wasn't going to get away with this. Gilbert and me, we were gonna have a little talk about what he'd done. Heck, he might've wound up getting me killed. What sort of person does such a thing in order to win a stupid contest?

I'd already said his name, hadn't I? No use in repeating it.

"Come on, Clem," Norma Ray said, opening the car door. "Let's get going."

"Y'all go on. I'm gonna walk home. It's not that far."

Malene's eyes flared with worry. "You sure? There might be a creeper lurking out here, and I don't mean the kind in Minecraft."

How did Malene know about the creepers in Minecraft? Okay, things I did not want to know the answer to. I pulled my phone from my pocket. "I've got this on me. In case anyone suspicious tries anything, I'll call Tuney Sluggs and have him come out in his pajamas to scare him off."

"Sounds like a plan," Norma Ray said. "Now come on, Urleen. Chauffeur me to my house."

Urleen rolled her eyes. "It would be my pleasure," she said, less than enthusiastically.

I laughed and waved as they drove off. It was a nice night, and I didn't mind being out in it. Once I got home, I'd have to call Rufus and let him know what happened with the mystic. *Rufus.* Okay, so at first yes, my feelings had been hurt about his whole not-wanting-to-do-things attitude, but it was slowly but surely beginning to grow on me. This could be good for us. It would mean that we'd have time to make sure that our relationship was on stable footing. We'd only been dating a few months anyway. What was a few more years?

A jolt of shock worked up my back. Years? Could it actually be that long?

No, Clem. Put that thought right out of your head. Goodness, if my life was a romance novel, folks would close the book and never re-open it. *Years.* As if.

Thinking about Rufus gave me time to cover good ground. Before I knew it, I was standing in front of Gilbert Wilcox's house. The lights were on, which meant someone, namely Gilbert, was home.

The more I thought about what Gilbert had done, the angrier I got.

Okay, I had to calm down and come up with a script—what exactly I would say.

This could take a minute.

My initial thought was, *Gilbert, you rat jerk, how could you put that mystic gnome in my yard?*

For some reason I had the feeling that beginning the conversation by insulting him might not get me anywhere. Okay. So it would be best not to do that.

How about, *Gilbert, I know it was you who planted that horrible gnome in my yard. If you're not careful, I'm going to put him in your closet so that it curses you.*

That was better, but still not exactly on track. There had to be a balance between forceful, firm and mean. It was like being a dog—you had to growl so that folks knew you meant business, but you couldn't just go around biting everybody or else you'd be put down.

Know what I mean?

It could be best to go into this whole thing playing dumb. *I don't know what happened, but someone stuck a cursed gnome in my yard. If I ever find out who did it, I'm going to make sure that gnome winds up at their house and never leaves.*

That was close enough to perfect to wing the rest. Be firm but nice, gauge his reaction and go from there.

All righty. I had a plan, and I was ready to take action. I stormed up Gilbert's steps. My nerve endings were on fire, sparking like crazy. Confronting people always made me nervous. I hated having to tell anybody something negative. It made me break out into hives.

Speaking of, my neck was already itching.

I resisted the urge to scratch it as I reached his front door. After giving it a good, hard knock, I waited for Gilbert to answer.

But no one came.

Maybe he wasn't home after all. I knocked one more time, just for good measure, but still the same outcome—no Gilbert in his tighty-whities answering my call.

"Well, that was a bust." I turned to leave when movement caught my attention. My gaze locked on a dark shape in the bushes. "What is that?"

I tiptoed over—do not ask my why. It wasn't like Gilbert was home.

But I guessed after the last time I was caught at his house, you know, when he called the police on me, I was a bit gun-shy.

There were still gnomes sprinkled all over his lawn. Dodging them was like walking across a minefield. The shape loomed up ahead but was cast in shadow. A wind picked up, making the hedges move, but the blob barely wafted with it.

When I was only a few feet away, I pulled out my phone and flipped on the flashlight.

I gasped. It was obvious what I was looking at. Someone was draped over the bushes, their back to me. Sticking out of their spine was a gnome, that had been shoved, hat first, into the person like a knife.

The body was a man, and I had a feeling that I knew which one. My hand shook as I reached out and took hold of his shoulder. It gave easily, as if the body was just dying to be turned over. Get it, *dying*?

Bad pun, I know.

The hedges offered some spring, and the body catapulted toward me before sliding to the ground. I screamed as my beam caught the man's face.

It was Gilbert. He had been impaled by one of his own gnomes.

And poor Gilbert was now very, very dead.

CHAPTER 18

"So this is how you found him?" Earl Granger asked.

Earl Granger was Tuney Sluggs's smart deputy. If Tuney was a hothead who literally labeled every murder an accidental death, then Earl Granger was the intelligent one who didn't.

Earl was tall with a mostly bald head except for a bit of fringe that wrapped over his ears and around the back. He had a little bit of a belly, but looked mostly fit for a man in his forties.

I gestured to Gilbert's dead body. "When I arrived, he was slumped over the hedges."

Lights had been placed all over the crime scene, turning night to day. A crowd had arrived, neighbors in their robes, and they stood on the sidewalk, hoping to get a glimpse of what was going on.

"I turned him over," I explained to Earl, "to see who it was, and that was when he fell. I was on my way back from a house I bought, and wanted to talk to Gilbert."

"About what?"

Crap. Here was the part that made me look guilty. "About the fact that I believed he had placed a very bad object in my yard, one that could do me harm."

Earl frowned. "What was the object?"

I sighed. "A gnome that tells the future but is really cursed."

Earl stared at me for a beat as if waiting for me to say that I was just kidding. When I did not, he scribbled something into the notebook he held. Probably, *Clementine Cooke suffers from delusions.*

Just kidding.

Not really.

"Anyway, I came over here and was about to leave when I noticed a shape and found out it was Gilbert."

Earl finished writing. "Do you mind staying around for a few minutes in case I have more questions?"

"I don't."

I moved off to the side as a dark SUV came flying down the street—Rufus. I'd called him after contacting the police. He parked and got out, striding across the road with steps steeped in determination.

As soon as he reached me, Rufus took me in his arms. "Are you okay?"

I nodded. "Yes. I'm fine."

His hands were warm on my shoulders, leaving imprints of heat when he finally pulled away and held me at arm's length. His gaze was full of concern, searching me.

"Gilbert?"

"Dead. Impaled by one of his own gnomes."

"Could it have been an accident?"

I shook my head. "I don't think so. Not the way he was positioned."

"And you're the one who found him? This doesn't look good."

"What do you mean?"

He quirked a brow. "News travels fast in Peachwood. I've already heard about his outburst at the ceremony today."

I laughed bitterly. "That's not the worst of it."

His brow wrinkled with worry. "How so?"

I went on to explain about the mystic and how the old lady gang and myself had worked magic to get rid of it.

"And did you?" he asked. "Manage to vanish the thing?"

"Yes," I said proudly. "Did you know that Malene keeps a banishing spell in her house?"

"Nothing Malene does surprises me. I wouldn't be shocked if she kept the recipe for starting a new universe in her purse."

I laughed. "No, that would be Urleen, not Malene. Urleen keeps just about everything in her handbag. She's like Mary Poppins."

"Right. Listen, you've had quite a shock. I don't want you to be alone tonight."

He hesitated, like a really long time. So I thought I'd help him out. "Do you want to come over? Stay the night?" Rufus hedged. Did I have food between my teeth? Last I'd checked, I hadn't asked if he wanted to marry me. "Promise I won't try anything."

"Is it okay if I do?"

Was it okay? Did the sun rise in the east?

But instead of blurting that out, I played it cool. "Yeah, it's fine. I mean, my bed is big enough for the two of us. You can stay in my room if you need to, but like I said, I'll keep my hands to myself. But now that I think about it, this whole situation will probably give me nightmares. It would be best if you did, actually, stay in my bed. I might need to reach out to you to snuggle. Is that okay?"

His lips curled with worry. "Clementine Cooke, are you trying to get me to turn my back on my values?"

"Absolutely not. But if your values want to take a small vacation for a night, that would be okay."

He shook his head, chuckling. "They're not taking a vacation. Trust me, one day you'll thank me for what I'm doing."

When I'm dead?

Which actually sent a chill down my spine. "There's something I haven't told you."

"What's that?"

"I took one of the fortunes from the mystic. Everyone did the other day, those of us who were there. The fortunes came true. All of them did."

"Has yours?"

"I don't know." A knot formed in my throat. I swallowed it down. "There was only one word written on it, and that was 'death.'"

"Death? I wouldn't put too much stock in it." He gestured to the police officers milling about the scene. "It might not have even been referring to you. You just witnessed a death. Well, you didn't actually *see* it, but you found the victim. Gilbert is dead. That is a death." Rufus rubbed my shoulder. "It's nothing to worry about."

But the expression on his face suggested otherwise. Either the card was something to be concerned with, or my boyfriend was worried about a different thing, perhaps one that involved Sykes Laffoon.

That made more sense.

But I still couldn't push away the fear creeping up my throat. I couldn't explain it, but I had a feeling that the card the gnome had spat out was about me. That one way or another, death was coming for me, and I didn't know what to do about it. There was no way to cheat death, no way to outrun it. Sooner or later it came for us all.

I was just thinking that when a bang, louder than a gunshot, grabbed my attention. Someone had been shot. Someone nearby. I turned to see who had been hurt, and that was when all heck broke loose.

CHAPTER 19

Juney Sluggs slammed on the brakes of his car, which had just backfired. That was the gunshot that I thought I'd heard. I exhaled a deep breath and relaxed. My fingers uncurled from Rufus's shirt. I hadn't even realized that I'd grabbed him.

Sluggs climbed out of his vehicle, wearing—you guessed it—his bathrobe and cowboy boots. But no hat. Strange.

Like, was that all he owned at home? Just a bathrobe, boxers and boots? Why didn't the man bother putting on one stitch of clothing to head outside? What was wrong with him?

A lot, apparently.

Earl Granger motioned for Sluggs to come over, and the chief did so. They spoke for a few minutes, during which time Earl pointed to me. Sluggs's gaze pinned in my direction. As much as I wanted to believe that he was admiring my hair, which had looked really great today, it was much more realistic that Sluggs was eyeing me as the initial suspect in their brand-new murder case.

After talking to Earl, the chief came over, just like I thought he might. "Do I need a lawyer?" I joked to Rufus.

"He probably just wants to ask you a few preliminary questions."

"He always thinks I'm guilty of something," I whispered.

"Nonsense. You found the body."

"This week Gilbert and I had gotten into it," I reminded Rufus. "Things could look bad for me."

He shook his head. "Out of all the people here, you had less reason to want Gilbert dead than anyone."

"Clementine Cooke," Sluggs said in a commanding tone as he sauntered over, robe blowing back in the wind. "What brought you over to Gilbert Wilcox's house so late at night?"

Yep, he thought I was guilty all right. "Like I told Deputy Granger, I came over to talk to Gilbert about something he left on my lawn."

Sluggs lifted one bushy eyebrow in question. "Was it a steaming pile of dog doo?"

"What? No. It was a gnome."

"You just won the contest, isn't that right?"

I rolled my eyes. "You know that I did. You were there when Jackson Briscoe handed me the trophy."

Sluggs hooked his thumbs into the belt of his robe and leaned back, all confident like. "And isn't it true that you and Gilbert got into a fight?"

"No, that is not true." Did he have dementia? "Gilbert screamed and yelled because I'd won. He was a sore loser. If you don't recall, there was a fistfight right here in this very yard only a couple of days ago. And if you also remember correctly, I had nothing to do with said fight. That was between Wallace, Jackson and Gilbert. He started the whole thing."

"So you say," he said suspiciously.

Rufus's jaw clenched. "I'm sorry, Chief Sluggs, but you don't actually think Clementine might be involved in Gilbert Wilcox's death, do you? She came upon his body, his back to her, a gnome thrust into it, and she called the police. She called your men to come and investigate. If she was actually guilty of a crime, don't you think she would have run away like a coward? Doesn't that make more sense?"

Sluggs tapped his temple. "We don't know the minds of criminals."

"Actually, you do," Rufus told him. "It's called criminal behavior. I'm fairly certain there are many courses taught on the subject."

"Oh," was all Sluggs could think to say.

From behind us, Malene's voice rang out. "Tuney Sluggs, just what do you think you're doing with my granddaughter?" She strode up the sidewalk with Willard trailing behind her. "You release her right now and let her go home. She's already had enough of a shock. She doesn't need you adding to her stress."

Oh no. Could this get any worse? Malene had dragged Willard here? What in the world was she thinking?

She wasn't; that was the truth of it.

"Malene Fredericks, what do you want?" Sluggs demanded.

She stopped a few feet away and crossed her arms. "I have heard through the grapevine that you were accosting my Clementine, and I came to stop it."

"Well, your granddaughter found a dead body," he told her.

Willard patted the air and said in a grandfatherly way, "Why don't we all just calm down a bit? This is a very emotional situation. Gilbert's dead. It's all highly suspicious."

Sluggs cast a narrowed eye on Willard. "What do you know about it, Gandy?"

"Well, um, I…just what the neighbor women have called Malene saying."

Sluggs, not to be deterred, glared at him hard. "Oh, is that right?"

Willard's cheeks puffed out in anger. "Now I didn't come all this way down here to be treated like a criminal. You and I both know that Clementine doesn't have a mean bone in her body."

"Yeah, Sluggs," Malene snapped, her head snapping right and left, "why don't you go and do what you do best—declare that Gilbert accidentally died, that somehow he fell onto a gnome and then managed to heave his big fat body on top of a row of bushes?"

Amazed at her depth of knowledge, I said, "You know all that about the crime?"

She smiled bashfully. "The neighbor women see a lot. They gave me all the details when they called." I glanced over at the folks still watching the scene from the street. "Not them." Malene pointed to the surrounding houses. "Them. They're the ones who contacted me."

Sure enough, when I glanced up at the homes, curtains were quickly drawn. No one wanted to be accused of spying on the police proceedings going on below.

Malene slipped her arm through mine. "Now, if you don't mind,

Sluggs, I will be taking my granddaughter home. She's already had enough to deal with, considering that Gilbert tried to curse her."

"I knew it," Sluggs exclaimed. "I knew she had a reason for wanting him dead."

That was it. I was sick and tired of the chief standing there accusing me. So I exploded. "I had no reason to want Gilbert dead. If anyone had a reason to stick a gnome in his back, it was you."

Malene and Willard gasped. Rufus slid a hand down his face as if suggesting that I'd done it now. Well, maybe I had, but I didn't care.

I went on. "Let me remind you that the other night, when Gilbert accused me of attempting to sabotage his yard, that he also said that he would make sure that you never got reelected if you didn't do what he said."

"Actually, he said that his law office wouldn't support me," Sluggs corrected.

"Whatever!" I threw my hands in the air. "Same thing. Everyone in this town knows you love showing up to crime scenes in your bathrobe. You must have some weird sadistic fetish about it. What would you do if you weren't the worst police chief Peachwood had ever seen? Sit all by your lonesome watching reruns of *Gunsmoke* in your boxer shorts every night? You couldn't have that, now could you? No. You've got to run all over town accusing innocent folks of crimes. Or worse, pretending a crime doesn't exist where one does."

Everyone went silent. Even the officers a few yards away. All gazes were locked on me, and I didn't care. I'd finally told Tuney Sluggs what I thought of him, and it felt good.

Of course, it could also land me in jail.

Maybe I should have thought my tirade through before I let loose on him.

Before I had a chance to apologize, Earl Granger came over holding what looked like Tuney Sluggs's missing cowboy hat. Probably to arrest me. I grabbed hold of Rufus for protection. But Earl didn't turn to me. In fact, he looked right at Tuney Sluggs and ignored the rest of us.

"Chief, we found this at the crime scene."

Sluggs stared at the hat as if it had leprosy. "What's that doing here?"

Earl shook his head and pulled handcuffs from his back pocket. "I'm afraid you need to come with me."

Sluggs's gaze darted from the handcuffs to Earl. "What's going on here?"

His voice thick with regret, Earl continued, "I'm sorry, Chief, but I'm charging you for the murder of Gilbert Wilcox. You have the right to remain silent…"

Earl spoke, but I drowned out his words. All I could focus on was the surprise in Tuney Sluggs's face and the shock that he was being arrested.

CHAPTER 20

"All I know is that there's no way Tuney Sluggs killed Gilbert Wilcox," I said before shoveling a spoonful of chocolate chocolate-chip ice cream into my mouth.

Y'all, I was stress eating to the max, and I wasn't even the person who had been thrown into jail.

But anyway, Rufus and I were back at my house. He was keeping his promise to spend the night. We were both in the living room on the couch. I was eating, and he was watching me with what I can only describe as admiration for my ability to eat so quickly and yet not drop one glob of ice cream on my shirt.

Lady was also watching me. But she was doing so in the hope that a bit of the dessert would fall directly into her mouth. Since I was not about to kill my dog with chocolate, I was doing everything in my power to make sure that didn't happen.

Rufus raked his fingers through his dark hair. "I, too, have a hard time believing Tuney Sluggs would do such a thing."

"With a gnome, nonetheless," I said with a snort.

"Better a gnome than a knife," Lady quipped.

"I don't know. They're both bad."

Rufus rubbed my arm. "You've had quite a shock tonight. How about we put you to bed."

Even though I was elbow-deep in my gallon of Blue Bell, I put the lid back on. After all, any chance to have a private moment with Rufus won over ice cream any day.

Lady decided to stay in the living room as I cleaned the spoon and headed into my bathroom. I washed my face and brushed my teeth. When I came out, I gasped.

Rufus stood beside my bed wearing nothing but pajama pants. My mouth instantly filled with saliva. If I'd left my jaw open, I was pretty sure that I would have drooled on the floor.

"Wow, someone's ready for bed," I murmured.

Rufus pulled back the covers and gestured for me to climb in. "I just want to make sure that you are."

Not with him shirtless in my room, I wasn't. It took everything I had, but I managed to slip under the covers without attacking him.

He sat beside me, staring down. "You've had quite a day."

I ran my fingers up his arm. "I would like to have quite a night."

He chuckled, which didn't bode well for me. "I think the best thing for you is rest."

His chest was so tight, and his biceps could have been cut with a diamond they were so chiseled. If I had any say in it, Rufus was not walking out of this bedroom before sunrise. "I'm happy to rest. I'd just like some company is all."

He sighed. The sound was full of defeat. Good. I might actually win this argument. "I tell you what."

"Yes?" I asked brightly.

"I'll get under the covers for a little while."

"I'll take it," I blurted out.

I scooted over, and Rufus slipped in beside me, bringing with him a musky pine scent. I dug my nose into his chest and inhaled as his arm wrapped over me.

We laid like that for a few minutes. But then a bubble of tension built in my chest. I wanted to kiss him. I wanted to thread my fingers around his neck and pull him to me. Surely, he wanted that, too.

"I love you," he said, his fingers grazing my shoulder.

I pulled back and glanced up. "I love you, too."

Our gazes locked. The tension became so thick the room buzzed with energy.

That was when I made my move. I was tired of being good and waiting.

I pressed my lips to Rufus's, and he smooched back. His arms tensed around me for a moment, as if he was thinking that he shouldn't be kissing me, but then he made the right decision (in my opinion) and claimed my lips.

A moan escaped my lips. It seemed to excite him, because the kiss became deeper, longer. I brushed my hands down his chest to his belly. His stomach quivered at my touch.

Everything became heightened—our kiss, the heat wafting off his skin, the feel of his hands on me.

This was what I wanted. This was good.

His lips dropped from my mouth to nuzzle my cheek. "Oh, Clem, I love you."

"I love you."

And something right there, right then, broke the moment. Rufus stopped kissing me, and he slowly sat up.

Wait. What had I missed? Everything was good. We were kissing. We were heading in the right direction. Had I said the wrong thing? Should I take back the *I love you?*

"What's wrong?" I reached for him and entwined my fingers in his. "Did I do something?"

"No," he said quickly. "No. You didn't do anything. Absolutely noth-ing. You were perfect. It's me."

I scooted back and pushed myself up on the flock of pillows that sprinkled my bed. "Then what is it? You can't be serious about wanting to protect me. I can protect myself, you know. We've already come this far in our relationship. I'm ready to make the leap. I love you. You love me. What more is there?"

His eyes filled with sadness. "There is truth in that. I do want to protect you."

"From what?"

"From me."

His words sent a shock wave straight to my core. "What are you talking about?" I whispered. "Why would I need to be protected from you?"

Rufus glanced away, and his jaw clenched. "I don't want to hurt you."

"Are you planning to?"

"No," he said quickly. "Absolutely not. But I've never been in a relationship like this."

"What does that mean?" What did it mean? That he didn't like the relationship? That he was tired of it already? Tired of me?

"One where I deeply loved someone," he replied.

"Me neither," I admitted. "And I never expected it to be with you."

"What if…what if I can't give you what you want?"

"I don't understand."

He sighed heavily and rose from the bed. *No, I wanted to shout, don't leave the bed. Get back here!*

"You know my history," he explained. "I've lived my life not being a good person. What if that holds me back. What if it holds you back?"

"I don't understand."

Rufus pointed to his chest. "What if there's some sort of governor on me? A cap that only allows me to do so much good before I become selfish again?"

"I don't believe that," I told him. "That's not who you are."

"It's not who I am now. But what if something happens? Do people really change?"

"They do if they want to." I reached for him, but Rufus stood just beyond my touch. "You have come so far. You are not who you used to be. You are a kind, caring man. One who I love and who loves me—I think."

"More than you know," he whispered. "But I worry that my nature, my true nature is simmering beneath the surface, waiting to be released. And if it does, you'll get hurt. Very badly. I could not forgive myself if something happened to you because of me."

Oh, this was just nonsense. I flipped the covers off me and rose, striding to Rufus with long steps. I cupped his face in my hands and stared up at him. "You would not hurt me. I believe that. I know it."

"But I don't." He pulled my hands from his cheeks and stared down at me. Anguish blazed in his eyes. "I don't know what I'd do if I hurt you."

"Then don't."

He shook his head. "Every step we take in our relationship brings us one point closer to the ultimate goal. Tell me—what do you want?"

I frowned. "What do you mean?"

"Your goals in life."

"Have a successful business."

"What else?"

I knew where this was going, what he wanted me to say. Part of me didn't want to tell him just so I could claim not to want what everyone else did. But he'd see right through that.

I sighed, annoyed. "I want a family."

"And how do you plan to get that?"

"I don't know. I might wait until women are able to inseminate our children by ourselves, without the help of a man."

He shook his head. "You're stalling."

I threw up my hands. "Fine. I would eventually like to get married and have kids same as a lot of other people in the world. What's wrong with that?"

He took my shoulders gently. "Nothing is wrong with that. Absolutely nothing. That's a normal course in a relationship. People get married. They have children. Unless you're me, that is."

And that was when a heavy chord of fear struck in my heart. "What in the devil are you talking about?"

He shook his head sadly. "Clementine, I don't know if I can give you what you want. My heart was black. What if it still is, somewhere deep down?"

I peered into his eyes, looking for the inky darkness he swore was in there. "I don't see it. If it's there, the evil is doing a good job of hiding. Rufus, I have overcome my fears with you. I know who you are. If you don't, then I can't help you. Only you can help yourself."

He started to speak, but I wasn't finished. "The old Rufus is gone. If you're afraid of becoming him again, or that he lives somewhere deep inside of you, you're wrong. That other Rufus, the one who hurt so many people so long ago, has vanished. He's been replaced with you. You are the real person. The good one who's standing in front of me now. Yes, I want certain things out of life. But I think that maybe you do, too. Otherwise you wouldn't be with me. We both want those things —to be with each other. I've never had this connection with anyone before, not like I do with you. You can stand there and say that you're afraid that when I need you, you won't be present, but that's wrong. You've already stepped up so many times."

I flung my hand toward the window for emphasis. "If it weren't for you, I'd still owe Sykes Lafoon money. If it weren't for you, I wouldn't know how to really use my magic."

"Something you don't practice enough of," he reminded me.

"Thank you," I said sarcastically. "You have influenced my life and changed me. I love you."

"And I love you," he said sadly.

That was when I knew the conversation wasn't going to end well. I knew that all his doubts and fears, worries and insecurities about himself were about to rear their ugly heads in my life.

"I'm afraid that you are going to need more in life and I'll fall short," he told me.

"Did nothing I say matter to you? Did you hear anything that I just told you?"

"Of course I did."

"But you didn't listen. I can handle whatever you throw at me. I'm a big girl."

He tucked a loose strand of hair behind my ear. "You deserve to be happy. I don't know if I'm the person who can give it to you."

Anger bubbled in me. "Because of your fears? You're afraid of something that hasn't even happened yet? You're afraid of possibilities."

"I'm only looking out for you." The sadness that filled his eyes made my heart want to explode. "I wish you could see that."

"What I see," I said, fuming, "is a man who wants to take the best relationship he's ever had and throw it out the window."

He started to argue but stopped. His hands fell to his sides, and Rufus took a step away. "Maybe I should go."

"I think that would be best."

I didn't follow as he walked from the room, but I heard the clap of magic as he dressed himself and unlocked my door. After he shut it behind him, Rufus used another thunderclap to bolt the locks back into place.

That was when I sank to my bed and cried.

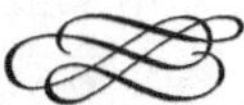

CHAPTER 21

I didn't sleep that night, and in the morning my stomach was sour as all get-out. Food didn't sound like a particularly good idea, so after feeding Lady, I skipped breakfast and headed out to my flip house.

At least that was one good thing in my life. The mystic gnome was gone, never to return. That part of things could get back to normal. Let's face it, after the night I'd had, I needed normal.

I mean, what was Rufus thinking? I never said that I wanted to jump into marriage and have kids. When had those words come out of my mouth?

Other than last night when he'd asked about them, I meant. No, I'd never told him that I wanted to leap down the aisle. We'd only been dating several months. Granted, I loved him and yes, I could see myself spending the rest of my days with him. But that was neither here nor there.

I knew his darkness. I'd experienced it firsthand, and I'd forgiven him. Rufus wasn't the same person now that he'd been several years ago. He was better. I believed in him. Why couldn't he believe in himself?

I quickly realized that if I spent all day focusing on Rufus, I would go crazy, so I hopped into my truck and left. Yes, Lady remained at home because having to explain to her what happened with Rufus might wind up driving me nuts. She would go on and on and would probably blame me for his departure.

None of this was my fault.

Needless to say, I was relieved when I arrived at the house. Surely there was a wall or an old sink that I could smash to bits. If there was one thing that made me feel better on any given day, it was demolishing objects. It was hard to explain how smashing things was freeing. But let's just say, don't knock it until you've tried it.

I entered the house through the front door and was slowly making my way to the back of it, mentally ticking off all the damage that I could do, when a form stopped me.

I stood in front of the mudroom, in the rear of the home, and stared. The last time I'd been in that room, it was empty. But now something very boxy sat inside.

Like, very boxy.

My hear pounded against my ribs because as I closed in, I realized exactly what I was staring at.

My feet hit the threshold, and I sucked air. Sitting smack-dab in the middle of my mudroom was the mystic. Yes, the thing Malene had banished was back, and the gnome simply smiled as if he'd won some unspoken competition for survival.

I wanted to smack that grin right off its porcelain face.

My first thought was to call Rufus, but seeing as how I was not speaking to him, I instead called Malene.

She answered on the first ring. "What's wrong?"

"Don't I even get a hello?"

"Nobody calls this early unless it's Willard, and he's already here."

"Good to know," I replied, not wanting to go into Malene's private life. "But we have a problem." I told her what I'd found.

"Come on back here, and we'll figure something out."

"You think I should leave it all alone?"

"Do you want to play with it?" she snipped.

"Good point. I'll be over in a jiffy."

So I locked up the house and was heading to my truck when I spied a familiar head of hair. Wallace was walking down the path to my house, glancing in my yard.

I waved to her. "Wallace!"

She clutched her chest in surprise. "Oh, Clem! You scared me."

"Sorry." My purse slipped from my shoulder, and I hoisted it back up. "I was just inside and am on my way home. What're you doing over here?"

"Well, I was coming by to look at your gnome arrangement, but I see you've taken it down."

"Yeah, I've had some problems with it. Hey, did you hear what happened to Gilbert Wilcox?"

"No."

I dropped my voice. I don't know why. No one else was around. "He was murdered. Last night."

She gasped. "No. What happened?"

"Stabbed in the back with a gnome. Earl Granger took Tuney Sluggs into custody."

Wallace shook her head. "Gilbert's office always supported Sluggs whenever he was up for reelection, but I can't imagine what would have pushed the chief to commit murder."

"I know. He wears his pajamas anytime there's a night call."

She chuckled. "Yes. Oh, I just can't believe it. Tuney Sluggs, a murderer."

I couldn't believe it, either, which was why I asked my next question. "Where were you last night around eight?"

Wallace fidgeted with her hair. "I was putting in my curlers. I know that most women in the world use curling irons anymore to set their hair, but I'm old-fashioned. I like rollers in mine. I find that the curl holds better when I sleep in them."

Okay, possibly a plausible explanation. But I wasn't finished. "You really hated Gilbert."

She scoffed. "Wouldn't you if he'd thrown you out with the dirty dishwater like he did to me?" Then Wallace quickly added, "But I didn't kill him. There was no love lost there, but I couldn't imagine him dead. That's just horrible."

Her eyes filled with tears, and part of me believed her. Even though she and Gilbert had their differences, perhaps she did genuinely feel bad at his death. I know that I did. No, I hadn't liked him, but I also hadn't wanted to find Gilbert hunched over a hedge bush with a gnome sticking from his back.

"Well, thank you for talking," I said. "I need to get going."

"Oh? So soon?"

My gut twisted in panic. "Yeah. I've got this…thing going on." If you called a gnome mystic that had a habit of bringing death to people a *thing*, that was.

I said goodbye to Wallace and headed over to Malene's. When I arrived, she was serving Willard a chicken pot pie—for breakfast. "There's plenty for you, Clem," my grandfather told me. "Pull up a chair."

Malene cut me a chunk and it looked delicious with all its little bits of carrots and potatoes and all that rich, yummy gravy and flaky crust, but my stomach was a full of knots after what had happened with Rufus.

I had no appetite. But seeing as I didn't feel like getting Malene involved in my business, I picked at the pie, nibbling on the edges of the crust.

"Now what's this you were telling me?" she asked.

"Oh, well, the mystic gnome is back. It showed up in my mudroom."

Malene spoke to Willard. "We worked a potion to get rid of it."

"Let me guess—it didn't work." He brushed crumbs from his chin. "You know, sometimes magic isn't always the answer."

"But the thing is magical," Malene argued. "Of course that's the answer. Everyone knows the thing is cursed. It told Clem that there was death in her future."

"Well, I don't know about that," Willard replied. "There was some death, wasn't there? Clem is the one who found Gilbert."

I considered this. "You're right. Maybe that was the death that the card meant. Maybe I'm not going to die at all."

Malene's eyeballs nearly popped out of her head. "Have you not listened to one word that I told you about that stinking gnome? It brings doom and gloom everywhere it goes. Bad things will happen. You mark my words. We've got to find a way to get rid of it and for good."

"Then we need answers," Willard said. "And since you didn't get a resolution by banishing it, I suggest you look somewhere else."

"Where's that?" I asked.

Willard rubbed his chin in thought. "You know, didn't Jackson Briscoe used to trade in magical objects of some sort? A long time ago?"

"Really?" I asked, surprised. Jackson Briscoe did not seem the type to be into magical objects. He appeared much too clean-cut for all that. Not that you had to be hippie-dippie in order to work magic. Not at all. He simply didn't fit my idea of a Peachwood wizard.

Well, let's face it—when it came to Peachwood wizards, I didn't have much luck. I mean, Rufus basically ran screaming from any kind of future with me, and I hadn't pegged Jackson as having any magical abilities at all.

Would wonders never cease?

"I do believe you're right," Malene said. "But I think he *collected* magical objects more than anything else. He never had his own store."

My brows raised in question. "So he's a collector?"

"From what I remember." Willard poked his chicken pie with a fork. "And a darn good one, at that. He'd be worth talking to. He may have an idea about how to get rid of it."

Malene and I exchanged a look that suggested we were thinking the same thing. She was the one who spoke, though. "He might also have an idea about who placed that gnome in your yard to begin with."

"How do you see that?" Willard asked.

"Because that person might've asked him questions. Or they could have told him," she snapped. "I don't know. It's a possibility."

Willard dropped his napkin beside his plate. "You've barely touched your food, Clem. You not feeling well?"

"I'm fine. Really. My stomach's just a little upset, that's all."

Now it was Malene and Willard's turn to exchange a look. "What is it?"

Malene shook her head. "Nothing. If you don't want to tell us what's really bothering you, then you don't have to."

"Thank you," I said pertly. "But since I've got this whole gnome thing on my mind, I'd like to head on over to Jackson's and see if he has time to talk. After all," I added in the chipperest voice I could muster, "there's no time like the present."

Willard pushed back his chair and rose. "Tell you what, I'll come with you. I've got some errands to do around town and could use with stretching my legs a little bit. You don't mind the company, do you?"

Well, I did want to be alone so that I could deal with my sorrows. But I hadn't spent any time with Willard recently, and being with him could cheer me up a bit.

Maybe.

"Oh, and I'd like to stop by the jail and see Tuney Sluggs," Willard said. "See how he's holding up."

"He can't be doing well with his own men thinking that he's a killer," Malene said sadly. "I never thought that Sluggs had it in him."

"I don't think he did," Willard said. "I believe that Tuney was set up."

My jaw dropped. "By who?"

"I don't know." Willard dusted a few remaining crumbs from his pants. "But I aim to find out. Come on, Clem. Let's go talk to Jackson and see if we can figure out how to get rid of your gnome problem, and then we'll see Tuney and find out if he remembers anything unusual about last night."

Impressed with him, I said, "Willard Gandy, I never took you for a sleuth."

He grinned. "It's time you got to know me better."

I linked my arm through his. "I would say that you're right."

CHAPTER 22

Jackson Briscoe happened to be home when we arrived. The outside of his home looked like it belonged on the cover of a magazine. It was all white rose arbors and azalea bushes, and there was even a fountain in the middle.

"I wonder where his moat is?" I asked Willard as we walked up the steps.

"Huh?" my grandfather said.

"Never mind."

But Rufus would have gotten my joke. He probably would have said that the moat was in back with the serfs, who were the ones making the yard look so good.

I really missed Rufus, and it had only been twelve hours since we'd broken up. How was I going to get through this day and all the rest without missing him something fierce?

I steeled myself. I would take things one day at a time. That's what I'd do. It was exactly what was called for, and I could do it. Yes, I could.

Couldn't I?

Anyway, Jackson answered the door in his houndstooth jacket. Surprise registered on his face before he thrust out his hand and shook the one Willard had extended.

"Willard, haven't seen you in a while. What brings you here?"

My grandfather nodded to me. "Seems my granddaughter here has a problem."

His mouth pursed in worry. "Clementine, is everything all right?"

"Why don't we come in?" Willard suggested.

"Of course." Jackson moved out of the way, giving us room to cross the threshold. "Please excuse the mess. I haven't had time to pick up this morning. The entire town's buzzing about what happened last night."

"To Gilbert?" Willard asked.

"Yes. No one can believe it."

Jackson's house, much to my surprise, was immaculate. There wasn't a thing out of place. I have no idea what he'd been talking about when he said that there was a mess, but the place was stellar. Even the carpet was free of lint. I probably could've eaten off his floor.

And it wasn't just that the place was beautiful, with lots of dark walnut built-in shelves and wood so freshly polished that the air still held a bit of the scent of orange from the Murphy's oil soap that Jackson had used. It was that tucked inside all the shelves were objects —curios, if you would.

There were dolls and antique toys—a sailing boat with faded blue paint, a wind-up monkey holding cymbals, a wooden train. There was also an African tribal mask, pottery, a jewelry box and many more items.

"What are all of those?" I asked.

Proudly Jackson said, "These are my collections. For years I've dabbled in acquiring magical objects, and here are some of what I've gathered."

I approached the monkey with the cymbals and couldn't help but be repulsed by the sneering smile. "Are they safe?"

He chuckled. "They're as safe as they can be. They may be magical, but they're not cursed, if that's what you mean."

"Yes, it's what I meant."

Willard spoke. "Jackson, the reason why we've come unannounced is because Clem has a little problem."

"The mystic gnome," Jackson said.

My jaw dropped. "You know about it?"

"I couldn't help but spot it the day that we judged your yard."

Frustration coursed through me. "If you knew about it, why didn't you do anything? Say something?"

Jackson pointed to a couch. "Please sit."

Willard and I did as he asked, but the whole time I was fuming. If Jackson had known about the gnome, he should have said something. He shouldn't have left me with that creature.

Willard dropped his hands between his knees. "What do you know about it?"

"I know that it's supposed to be cursed, is what. I thought that the gnome in your yard looked familiar, but it wasn't until I did some research on it that I discovered for sure what it was. I returned to your house this morning to talk to you about it, but the gnome was gone. I assumed you'd gotten rid of it."

"We did. Or at least I thought so, but it's come back."

Jackson gave me a stern look. "So it wasn't you who called it in the first place."

"Heavens, no. I didn't even want to compete in the golden gnome. This competition leads to murder."

Jackson shook his head. "It did this time. I'm afraid after all my years of competing, I've donated all my gnomes. They simply took up too much room in my shed. But anyway, that's neither here nor there. You are the one with the problem."

"I need that thing gone."

He nodded, sympathy filling his gaze. "The only way to get rid of it is to get the person who called it in the first place to send it back to where it came from."

My heart stuttered. "What? But I don't know who that is."

Jackson gave me a sad smile. "I'm afraid that until you find out, you're stuck with it."

"Isn't there another way?"

Jackson shook his head. "I don't believe so, no. But tell you what—I can come up with some ideas, see if my research reveals anything. If an idea comes to me, I'll give you a call. What's your number?"

I gave him my number even though my heart sank. The only person who could get rid of the gnome was the same crazy random person who had put it there in the first place? But who had that been?

"You don't happen to know who did this to me, do you? Has anyone spoken to you about any magical objects?"

Jackson shook his head sadly. "No, not at all."

Either he was lying or he wasn't, and I had no reason to believe that Jackson would lie.

Gosh, I really hoped Gilbert hadn't been the person who stuck me with that mystic. I'd never get rid of it if that was the case.

We thanked Jackson for his help and left. As we were climbing into Willard's truck, he said, "Do you get the sinking feeling that Gilbert's death and the gnome in your yard are connected?"

No, I hadn't, at least not until that moment. "What makes you say that?"

He paused, keeping one hand on the door while speaking to me over the hood of the vehicle. "The way I see it, it's got to be more than a strange coincidence that you were suddenly given a wonderful gnome arrangement, one that would ensure that Gilbert didn't win this year. And then right after the winner is announced and Gilbert cries foul, he winds up dead by a gnome. Doesn't all of that seem strangely coincidental?"

"But then why give me the gnome? I didn't want it."

Willard tapped the door in thought. "Maybe you weren't supposed to get it. Perhaps the person was going to set it in Gilbert's yard but for some reason or another, couldn't. So they stashed it on your lawn, intending to get to Gilbert the whole time." He rubbed his chin. "The more I think of it, the more it makes sense. It's not you who had the enemy here. It was Gilbert. You just wound up in the crosshairs, Clem."

"Well, I'd like to be taken out of the crosshairs, if you know what I mean."

He nodded. "I do. Tell you what, let's go get ourselves a coffee from Julie's. My treat. Oh, and we'll take one to Tuney, see if it lifts his spirits a little."

"I don't know about him, but one of Julie's mochas always lifts my spirits."

Willard slid onto the seat. "Well, come on then. What are we waiting for?"

~

THE MOCHA from Julie's was amazing, if I did say so myself. She served us with a big smile, as she always did.

"How're things going, Clem?"

Her dark curls were tied back, though a few still sprang around her face. Julie was practically glowing. There was a new man in her life, and I had a feeling he was the reason why. But since I didn't want to get into my own life, I just smiled and said things were good.

When we had our drinks, Willard pointed to a table. "Let's sit. I'm not good at sipping hot drinks and driving. I always end up with spills. Besides, I've still got to order something for Tuney. We'll grab that before we leave."

We sat and of course the first thing that happened was Rufus walked in. Like, walked right into Bender's, saw me and stopped. He forced a smile and headed over.

"Willard, Clem. How're you today?"

"Good," I said curtly.

"Great to see you, Rufus." Willard shook his hand. "Why don't you sit for a spell?"

Rufus shook his head. "I'm sorry, but I can't. There's a spell I'm hunting. I only came to grab a quick drink."

"Don't let us stop you," I murmured.

Rufus held my gaze for a moment before saying goodbye and walking off. Heat blazed in down my cheeks and through my entire body. I didn't start to cool down until he left the building.

When he was gone, Willard said, "Do you want to tell me what that was all about? Or would you rather I guess and then be forced to spill a falsehood to Malene that she may or may not blab to every living person she passes on the street?"

I barked a laugh because that statement was mostly true. I ran a thumb across the coffee lid and sighed. "We broke up last night. Rufus said that he's not sure that he can give me what I want. He thinks that he'll turn all evil wizard on me or something."

"Hmm."

Willard sipped his drink. I think he was stalling for time so that he could think of the right words to say. I could've helped him there because there weren't any. Nothing would cheer me up.

"It's okay," I told him. "None of it is good."

"You can look at it that way," he said.

I laughed bitterly. "What other way is there to look at it?"

"Well, Rufus loves you. That much is obvious. And you love him. Given his history, he probably is worried that he'll do something to hurt you."

"Like breaking up with me?"

"Look, I don't know what goes on in his mind. I'd be lying if I said that I did. But I do know that he cares about you—a lot. It could be that he just needs time to see that. We men can be stubborn."

I shook my head. "But I don't want to be on a seesaw with him. If he changes his mind now, what does that mean for later? That something will scare him off again? I can't keep going through that. Either he wants to be with me or he doesn't. I know who Rufus is. He's battled his demons. At some point he has to put them to rest."

"I agree." Willard tapped a finger to his cup. "Maybe something happened that made him think that things were getting serious and he wasn't sure that he's ready."

"He says that he's trying to protect me."

"And I think that's the truth. Just give him time. And if he doesn't come around, then he wasn't the man you were meant to be with. Trust me, Clem. Whoever catches you will be one lucky guy, if I do say so myself."

He said it with such a warm smile on his face that it was contagious. "Thank you." I cupped a hand over his. "I appreciate it."

"Well, it's the truth. Now. You ready to head over to see Tuney?"

"Sure." And I meant it. Willard's words, though they didn't hold a solution, did lighten my heart. I felt better, ready to get going.

He bought a drink for Tuney Sluggs, and we left Bender's. We had just stepped outside. It was a warm day, and a cool breeze flitted around us, bringing with it the scent of honeysuckles. I was inhaling deeply, absorbing the smell, when the screech of car brakes filled the air.

They were followed by a scream.

Willard took my arm. "Come on."

We raced down the street. A crowd was gathered. Willard pushed his way through, and there I witnessed the horror.

The man who had first claimed that the mystic gnome was full of malarky, the one who had been told that he might be in an accident, lay dead on the street.

The driver of the car got out. "I don't know what happened. He just appeared out of nowhere."

But I knew what had happened. I knew all too well and realized exactly what my fate was going to be.

CHAPTER 23

I did my best to push my future from my head, but let me tell you that when you see a man hit by a car—a man who'd received a certain slip of paper from a horrible gnome foretelling that he needed to watch out for accidents—well, it was hard not to be scared out of my mind.

But as Tuney Sluggs was in jail for a crime that even I knew he hadn't committed, it seemed best to think less about myself (and my potentially imminent demise) and more about the chief of police.

Willard and I showed up at the station a little while later. Earl Granger wasn't in and the officer in charge didn't look too keen on letting us speak to the chief, but when I gave him a bit of sass and asked if Tuney had been told he couldn't have visitors, the officer meekly said that he could.

He led us back to the cells, and we found Tuney slumped atop his sad little cot that had brown stains (from who knows what) dripping down the sides of the mattress.

When he saw us, his eyes lit up like they were charged with a thousand watts. "Clem. Willard. What're y'all doing here?"

"We brought you a coffee," I said, handing him the cup through the bars.

"Oh, good. I spilled the last one. Couldn't keep my hands from shaking." Tuney pointed to the stains on the cot. Well, question answered. They were simply harmless coffee marks, not something much, much worse. "Thank y'all for coming."

"It's the least we could do," Willard said.

Tuney pointed to the wall behind us. "Pull up a chair. There's no one around. Y'all might as well sit a spell."

We pulled up two aluminum folding chairs. I threw myself into the conversation to avoid focusing on anything else. "I'm just going to jump in. How did your hat end up at the crime scene? I mean, I know you didn't kill Gilbert Wilcox. You can barely drive at night. I can't see you hurling a gnome into his back."

Tuney looked about halfway to angry at my comment about him being old and feeble, but instead of shouting at me, he shook his head sadly. "Well, I just don't know about my hat. I know that I had it on me when the winner of the golden gnome was announced. I remember having it, but I took it off around lunchtime because my head was sweating. See, I have a condition where I get a sweaty head every now and then."

Well, that was too much information. The last thing I wanted to hear about was Tuney Sluggs's perspiring pate. The thought made me want to retch.

"Where'd you have lunch?" Willard asked.

"At the country buffet. On Thursdays they have the best chicken and dressing. I don't care what time of year it is. I can always eat their dressing. I don't need a special occasion like Thanksgiving to indulge. That Rhonda over there—she is some cook."

I lifted my hand to make him stop. "Okay, before you get too over the top about Rhonda, back to the facts. That's the last time that you remember wearing your hat? Was there anyone else at the country buffet that you remember?"

Tuney scrubbed a hand down his cheek. "Well, I can't rightly say."

Willard spoke. "Tuney, we believe that there's a connection between a strange magical gnome that showed up in Clem's yard and Gilbert's death. Now, we don't know who did either. But we think that if we can pin down the perpetrator, he or she will be guilty of both."

"I see," Tuney said in a way that did not make me think he saw at all.

"So was there anyone at the country buffet that would have wanted to kill Gilbert? You know, he got into that fight with Wallace and Jackson a few days ago. Not that I think either of them would have done such a thing. But it could be possible."

Tuney considered my question for a moment. He thought and thought, and after a few seconds finally said, "Yes, I do remember seeing someone. Now that I think about it."

Willard and I exchanged a victory glance. "You did?" I asked. "Who was it?"

Tuney took a long sip of his coffee. It was so long that I was just about to tip his cup up so that he could finish the drink and get to talking. But as I ended my thought, he answered, "Well, let me tell you who I saw."

WILLARD and I left the jail with new information, information that neither of us had expected.

"What should we do now? Tell Earl Granger?" I asked.

My grandfather shook his head. "I'll speak to Earl and tell him. This may be the break they've been looking for."

"But what if he doesn't believe you?"

We were back at Willard's truck. He tapped the hood. "If I tell Earl what I'm thinking, that Sluggs was set up and that his hat going missing and the magical gnome are clues, he'll have to listen. But I've got to talk to him when he's relaxed. If I charge into his office demanding that he hear me, Earl might shut me out."

"Do you think he would do that?" A warm wind whipped by. It grabbed tendrils of my hair and threw them in my face. I scraped them from of my eyes with my nails. "Earl's always seemed really reasonable to me."

"There's a lot of attention going on with this case. Since Tuney's in custody, I imagine Earl's getting a lot of heat from several different directions. Tell you what—the deputy's medications are usually due in the pharmacy around this time of the month. I'll go grab them and drop them by his house this evening. That'll give me time to talk to him, tell him our theory."

Sounded like a winner to me. "Do you need my help? I'd be glad to come."

He smiled warmly. "Not this time. You've done a lot. Right now I just want you to relax. You've got enough on your plate."

Which was code for: this was man speak and no women were allowed. No, my grandfather wasn't the type to put females down. So I decided to trust his judgment.

"If you think that's best."

"I do. Come on. Let's get you home."

Once I was in his truck, I replayed in my mind what Sluggs had told us. "I just have a hard time believing that Jackson Briscoe would do such a thing. I guess it all makes sense. He does have a background in magical objects, and he had gotten into the fight with Gilbert. But why put the gnome in my yard? Why put me at risk? I'd never done anything to him. I just don't understand it."

Willard put the truck into drive, and we ambled down the road. "I don't know. The only person who does know is Jackson, and that's something for Earl Granger and his men to figure out. I'm just glad that we discovered what we did so that an innocent man won't have to rot in prison for a crime that he didn't commit."

"Yeah, Sluggs is much too old to go to prison. I don't think he'd last longer than a day in there."

"You and me both, kid."

I sank onto the seat and stretched my arms, relieved that this would all be over soon. Jackson would be hauled into jail, and of course he'd be forced to get rid of the magical gnome. My future would be secure, and all would be well again.

I hoped.

Yes, I know that I'd found Gilbert dead. So yes, he could have been the death that the gnome had predicted. But after seeing that man hit by the car today, I wasn't taking any chances. I wanted that gnome gone for good.

"You know," I said to Willard, "you and I make a good team."

"We sure do. We should do more sleuthing together. But I'd prefer we not do it when a murder had been committed."

I laughed. "What other time do we need to do it? I only stick my nose in other people's business when I sorely have to—and that is usually when someone's been killed."

"Or there's a black hole in Norma Ray's barn," he murmured, referring to an episode that had happened not long ago.

"That too," I joked.

He pulled up to my house. I thanked Willard and got out. But before I could disappear from view, he added, "Clem?"

"Yes, sir?"

"Try not to worry too much about Rufus. I know that's easier said than done. But if things are meant to be, then they're meant to be. Forcing it won't help matters."

A warm, fuzzy feeling filled the pit that had opened up in my stomach. "I'll do my best."

"Good girl. You gonna stop by Malene's tonight? Said she's making a pot roast."

"What's for dessert?"

He barked a laugh. "I don't know, but if I have anything to do with it, I'll make sure it contains chocolate."

"Then I'll be there with bells on."

He drove off, and I headed into the house. Lady accosted me first thing. "Clem, where have you been? I nearly starved to death."

I patted her silky head and pulled her into my arms. "I will have you know that I filled your bowl before I left."

"I know. It's been empty for hours," she whined. "I also have to pee like a racehorse. Why do they say that? *Pee like a racehorse?* Do racehorses pee a lot?"

I chuckled. "I have no idea. But they're big animals, so maybe when they go, they go a lot?"

"Makes sense. Take me outside or lose me forever," she said dramatically.

"Have you been watching *Top Gun* again?"

"Yes, I pushed the remote and it came on today. I just tear up at that movie every time I see it."

"You know that's a little steamy for you to be watching."

I put her down, and Lady scratched at the door. "I have no idea what you're talking about. I fall asleep during the kissing scenes. Boring!"

I laughed again before grabbing her leash and snapping it to her collar. "Come on. Let's go outside."

A few minutes later I had caught Lady up on all the goings-on in my life—including what had happened with Rufus and the whole Jackson Briscoe thing.

Lady, who I thought would be much more concerned about Rufus, only commented that he'd be back and I shouldn't worry about it. She also offered me sage advice such as, don't drink and dial, and don't answer when he calls me. Let him wait a bit and call him back a few hours or days later. Days, in her opinion, would be better than hours, but ultimately when I returned the call was up to me.

"What makes you think he'll phone?"

She rolled her eyes. "Y'all two belong together. He'll come around. You haven't put out, have you?"

I spit coffee onto the ground. "Um. No. And maybe you should phrase statements like that a little nicer."

She kicked up grass with her hind feet. "I didn't go to no fancy school. I speak the way I speak. End of story. But anyway, don't worry about him. But this whole Jackson thing sounds terrible. He put the gnome in your yard? My goodness, and then he killed a man? What is wrong with him? Why would he do such a horrible thing? Killing people is wrong. Don't he know that?"

"Yeah, but murderers don't care. They just murder…for whatever reason."

"What reason is that?"

I shrugged. "I really don't know. Maybe Gilbert kept on about losing the trophy. Maybe he told Jackson that he would ruin his career in some way, like he did to Tuney Sluggs. I have no idea. Only Jackson knows the answer."

"Well, when's he gonna tell?"

"Whenever Earl Granger hauls him in and gets him to confess."

"Hopefully that'll be sooner rather than later." She sniffed a tree before moving on. "But anyway, I'm looking forward to a nice evening with you. What're we gonna do?"

"Malene's making pot roast."

"Oh, my favorite. Will she make a plate for me?"

"Dog, that is human food. It's not good for you."

"I disagree. It's meat. It's vegetables. I watch those premium dog food commercials. That's all they have in them. No grains. I pay attention."

I laughed. "Okay, so maybe she'll give you a little bit."

"Thank goodness."

"But no dessert."

"I can live with that." She sashayed back toward the house. "You coming? We didn't lock the door behind us."

Her words triggered a memory. "Oh, wow. Yes, let's go. I just remembered something."

"What?"

"I forgot to lock the door to the flip house. I need to run over there real quick, and then we can head to Malene's. How does that sound?"

Lady narrowed her eyes. "You best hurry. I don't like it when things come between me and my stomach."

I plucked her from the ground and tucked her under one arm. "Don't worry. I won't let my life interfere with yours."

"Good. As long as you know that, we'll get along great."

I planted her back in the house, grabbed the keys to my truck and headed back out for what I thought would be a quick trip there and back.

Turned out, I was wrong.

Dead wrong.

CHAPTER 24

The whole time, on the trip over, I kept thinking about Jackson Briscoe and him murdering Gilbert Wilcox. Why would he have done that? Yes, they'd gotten into a fistfight and Gilbert had threatened to have him removed as a judge of the golden gnome, but was that enough to have committed murder?

I mean, really, was it?

There was something about it that simply didn't add up. Why would Jackson have killed Gilbert over something as trivial as judging? He had to be furious to shove a gnome in his back. It would have taken a lot of force, or even a world of anger to wield the gnome to the point where it became a weapon.

And the weapon itself was very telling. It was like the murderer was saying, *You want to be the golden gnome winner, Gilbert? Well, here you go.*

It was gruesome, really.

I wouldn't, not in a thousand years, think of hurting someone with a garden gnome. But then again, I wasn't a killer, now was I?

Good thing for that.

But even as I tried to brush aside the pesky thoughts, they still invaded my mind.

I could not, for the life of me, put my finger on it, but something told me that Jackson Briscoe might not be our man. Not wanting

Willard to make a fool of himself in front of Earl, I decided it would be best to call him.

I dialed his home phone, but no one answered. Where could he be? I'd just left him about half an hour ago or so. A thought hit me. What if he and Malene were…

Oh, gross. I nearly went mind blind from the thought. I would have to wash my head with bleach when I got home.

I arrived at the flip house a few minutes later. Promising myself that I would call Willard when I got home, I left my cell phone in the truck. After all, the only thing I needed to do was lock up the house and head on back. This shouldn't have taken but a minute.

I spied a few clumps of dirt where gnomes had uprooted the grass, and fixed them by locating chunks of fescue and forcing them back in the holes. I'd come back and water the yard tomorrow. That should help the grass set.

Goodness. Remind me never to allow Malene to put gnomes in my yard again. Oh, that's right. I didn't *allow* her to in the first place. My grandmother had simply done whatever it was that she wanted.

Of course she had. That was how Malene worked.

Sighing in frustration, I left the yard and headed toward the house. Wanting to make sure that I hadn't left anything inside, like a useful tool, I went in through the mudroom, planning to search the house from back to front.

But that plan went all to heck when I entered to find someone standing in my mudroom, right in front of the magical mystic.

"Wallace?"

She slowly straightened. Wallace turned and smiled. "Why, hello, Clem."

"What are you doing here?" Then I saw a book of magic lying beside the mystic. My eyes popped wide. "Oh no."

Wallace smiled shyly. "I can explain."

"No, I don't think you can. You are the one who called the mystic. You put it at my house. Which means"—I sucked air when I probably should've just kept my mouth shut—"you're the one who killed Gilbert Wilcox."

CHAPTER 25

*D*o not ask me how I knew. It was simply a sixth sense—plus it helped that Wallace had a magic book opened and was squatting in front of the gnome.

But she immediately flicked off my accusation. "I don't know what you're talking about. I would never have killed Gilbert. I lo-lo-lo—"

I rolled my eyes. "Please. Do not tell me that you loved Gilbert Wilcox. You hated him. You couldn't stand the man. He threw you out the door for that other little lady so that she could be his new paralegal."

She bunched up her fists. "All right! I hated him. Fine. Is that what you want to hear? I couldn't stand Gilbert Wilcox, and if I'd had my way, this mystical gnome would've ended his life instead of me."

Oh. Wow. There it was. The admission that Wallace had indeed killed Gilbert. Where was my cell phone when I needed it? That's right. It was in my car, in the front seat, waiting for me to return to it.

Boy, I had really played this whole scenario wrong. But maybe, just maybe I could get out of this. Perhaps if I slowly made my way out the back door Wallace wouldn't notice.

My fingers brushed the doorknob, and as I started to turn it, Wallace's eyes widened. She jerked her hand and pointed a knife at me.

Where in the world had she been hiding that?

As if she could hear my inner thoughts, Wallace said, "I need to spill some of my blood to get rid of the mystic."

"So you are trying to send it away?" At least I had that going for me. "Thank you."

"Don't mention it," she said. "I would've gotten rid of it sooner, but I couldn't find it. I assume you tried to banish it?"

"Yeah, we did. But it returned."

"That's the thing about cursed objects. They don't leave until the person who called them actually does the spelling."

"That's what I learned. But don't let me stop you. You can go ahead and send it off into the great unknown."

"While you escape and run to the police? I don't think so. Go stand over there."

She pressed back against the mudroom's wall so that I could slide by. I kept my back away from her, not trusting that she wouldn't shank me if I wasn't paying close enough attention.

"So, are you going to tell me why?" I asked.

She shrugged. "Why what?"

Oh, come on. Really? "Why you killed Gilbert. How and why?"

"Oh, well, I guess it all started when I wound up on the judging committee. I wanted him to fail, to fall flat on his face."

That I could believe. "So what'd you do?"

If I kept Wallace talking long enough, it could give me time to come up with a plan that would help me escape. I really, really needed to escape. Like, yesterday.

"I remembered something about a mystic gnome that had cursed folks before, so I tracked it down. It wasn't easy to locate that thing, let me tell you."

"I kind of wish you hadn't. A man who received a fortune from it died today."

Wallace's brown eyes flickered with sadness before she shrugged. "Sometimes in war there are casualties."

"I'm sorry, but this isn't exactly war."

Her eyes narrowed. "If you'd been through what I have, you'd disagree."

"Okay, so tell me."

"Gilbert used to treat me like a queen. I was his number one lady.

But then he fired me without reason, left me penniless. All he ever cared about was himself. So my plan was to plant the mystic in his yard. But while I was transporting it, people saw me. I had no choice but to dump it here, on your lawn. I meant to return and move it, but by that time everyone knew it was here."

I folded my arms. "Let me guess, so did Gilbert."

She nodded. "He guessed, realizing what I had planned, that my intention was to curse him. I was out walking by his house—I was thinking about throwing rotten eggs on it—but instead of that, we got into a fight. He said that he was going to tell everyone in town what I'd done, that I'd planted that mystic in your yard. He said that I'd be ruined in town. When he was done with me, I wouldn't be able to show my face anywhere."

Sounded about like something Gilbert would say. "So you killed him."

"When his back was turned, I grabbed a gnome and rammed it into his back. I didn't mean to kill him. I just wanted to hurt him. But you know what happened."

"I do."

There was a long pause while Wallace stared from me down to the knife she still unfortunately held. "And now I'm afraid that I have to end things. I like you, Clementine, I really do. But you can't live knowing what I've done. Don't worry, I'll get rid of the mystic gnome. You don't have to be concerned with that."

"Oh, well gee, thanks." As if that was my biggest concern at the moment. "I appreciate it."

She smiled brightly. "No problem. Now. If you'll just, um"—Wallace gestured for me to ram myself into the tip of the blade—"then we'll be all done here and I can get on with things."

I smirked. "As much as I would love to, there's just one problem."

"What's that?" she asked as if it hadn't occurred to her that any of this was strange and morally wrong.

"I have no intention of dying."

"Oh," was all she managed before I hit Wallace with a wave of magic that she had not been expecting.

She flew backward and smashed against the wall. I ran for the knife, but Wallace was fast, like superhuman fast. She reached the blade before me and swiped at my stomach. The tip grazed my shirt, slicing into the fabric.

"Hey, I really liked that shirt."

"You'll need to throw it out, now," she informed me politely. "Sorry. Listen, can't you just die easily, like Gilbert did?"

"You knifed him in the back," I screeched.

"Correction—I *gnomed* him in the back."

It would almost have been funny if it wasn't so dang morbid.

Wallace arched her hand in the air again, and this time I was ready. I hit her with another stream of magic. It missed her and connected with the knife, sending it clattering to the floor. Wallace didn't miss a beat. She charged at me, throwing her body into mine.

We both fell hard to the ground. The wind was knocked from my lungs. I couldn't think straight. I couldn't find my magic. My head was all clumped up with a thousand thoughts, but at the same time with none.

Wallace had her hands around my throat.

So I did the same to her, reaching up and wrapping my fingers around her neck.

"Stop it," she yelled.

"You stop it," I said through gasps.

That was when I found my magic. I supercharged my body and released an electric tidal wave that shot Wallace off me and into the wall, knocking her unconscious.

Gasping, I managed to get my shaking legs underneath me and forced myself into a standing position. Wallace's eyes were closed. She wasn't going anywhere soon.

I was about to head outside to retrieve my phone when the door banged open.

There stood Rufus.

I scowled. "What are you doing here?"

"I realized that Wallace was behind everything. I spoke to some people who saw her toting the mystic to your house. What's wrong?"

The worry in his eyes and voice made my heart break. I pointed to Wallace. "I know. We fought. I won."

Rufus looked like he wanted to rush over and wrap me into a hug. But he did not. "And you?"

"I'm fine. Thanks for showing up."

"I…" He crossed over and reached out. Turned out, he *was* going for the hug.

"Don't." I stepped back. "I don't need a consolation prize."

"I wasn't going to do that."

I scoffed. "Yes, you were. You were going to hug me because I almost got killed, not because you think we should be together."

"You can't read my mind."

I glared at him. "I can, too." Which was a total lie. "You didn't sweep over and take me in your arms like you would have if you hadn't broken up with me."

"I did that for your own good," he spat. Fire filled his eyes. "I'm sorry that trying to do something for you is so wrong."

"It is wrong when it—"

"When it what?"

Breaks my heart. But I wouldn't let him know that. He didn't deserve the satisfaction of knowing the depth of my feelings.

"Let's just call the police," I said. "Get Earl Granger out here so that Tuney Sluggs can be released."

I felt so deflated, wrung out. Rufus and I locked gazes. The sadness in his eyes squeezed my heart until it was nothing but a twisted rag.

He slowly nodded. "I'll make the call."

"Thank you."

"You're welcome."

And he did. Rufus and I waited in silence while the sounds of police sirens filled the air, coming to arrest a still very unconscious Wallace.

CHAPTER 26

*I*t turned out that I suppose the mystic had been right about one thing—there had been death in my future. I'd found Gilbert, and Wallace had attempted, unsuccessfully, to murder me.

Which I supposed meant that the gnome's foretellings weren't always accurate, thankfully.

I also discovered that the woman who'd been given the fortune of meeting a new love had indeed really been blessed by the mystic. She and her new beau were already talking about walking down the aisle.

I could not say the same about myself, of course.

"Come on, Clem," Malene called. "The girls'll be here any minute."

"Coming!" I stepped out of Malene's back door and into her yard holding a bowl of potato salad. "What time did you say everyone was arriving?"

Malene settled a plate of barbecued pork on the table atop her pretty pink eyelet cloth and smiled with admiration. "They should be here any minute."

"Malene, what can I grab?" Willard called from behind the screen door.

"The plates! Get the plates," she called.

"Am I early?" a voice boomed from behind us.

We turned to see Tuney Sluggs standing fully dressed in slacks, a shirt, his cowboy hat and boots. He smiled widely, and Malene rushed over.

"No, you're not early. Everyone should be here soon."

He wrapped her in a hug. "Thank you for throwing this party for me."

"Aw, it's the least we could do to celebrate your release from jail."

"Makes an old man feel appreciated."

Malene grinned. "You are appreciated. Oh, I forgot something. I'll be right back."

She rushed off into the house, and Sluggs headed toward me. "Clem, I can't thank you enough."

"For almost dying?" I joked.

"No, none of that. For believing in me. It means a lot."

I rubbed his shoulder. "I'm glad that you're not so bad, after all."

He placed a withered hand over his heart. "And from now on, I will not look at you suspiciously, and if someone dies under less than innocent circumstances, I will believe that it could be murder."

I barked a laugh. "Boy, jail must've really done a number on you."

"That it did. To have my colleagues believe I could commit such an atrocity was certainly mind-blowing."

His words hit me in the spine. "Well, I know Earl Granger feels awful about it."

Sluggs only nodded.

Norma Ray's voice came from the street. "Is there supposed to be a party here? Where're all the guests?"

I laughed as she waddled up with Urleen in tow. "It looks like y'all are just beginning to arrive."

"Good," Norma Ray said. "'Cause I've got my good Spanx on. I can stand all night."

We all laughed as more and more folks arrived.

And yes, Rufus was also on the guest list. I managed to avoid him for most of the evening but eventually found myself at the dessert table when he walked over.

My mouth watered at his appearance. His dark hair was swept back from his eyes. He wore a white button-down and black suit that fitted him as if it had been tailor-made. His cheekbones popped in the light, making them look razor-sharp, and his full lips were begging to be kissed.

But not by me.

"Clementine." My name fell from his mouth like a velvet carpet unfurling. "It's good to see you."

Every nerve in my body jacked up. I had always been told that if I didn't have anything nice to say, I shouldn't say anything at all. But I had to say something.

"You look nice," I told him.

"You look gorgeous," he replied. "Is that a new dress?"

It was, but he didn't need to know that. "This old thing? No. It's been in my closet forever."

"So...how are you?"

"Great." It came out forced. I wasn't great. I was miserable without him. "And you?"

"Doing fine. Keeping busy."

Note, the entire time our backs were to the table and we were both looking out and watching everyone. We were not making eye contact. I was pretty sure that if our eyes locked, we'd both burst into flames.

"That's good," I murmured. "The keeping-busy part, I mean."

And then he said it. "I've missed you."

My breath hitched. I swallowed a knot in the back of my throat. I'd missed him something awful. But it wouldn't help to keep tearing at our relationship wound and letting it bleed all over the place. I'd never heal if we did that.

"I've... It's good to see you, too. I need to go."

Before he could utter another sound, I walked away. I don't know what Rufus wanted, but he was the one who'd said that he couldn't give me what I wanted. No, I didn't want to be reminded of that every few seconds, so yes, I left.

I headed around to the front of the house, looking for air. I needed to breathe. I closed my eyes and inhaled and exhaled. Inhaled and exhaled until I felt better.

After a few minutes my heart rate slowed and calm took over me. I opened my eyes.

A strange man stood in front of me. He was tall and lean, muscular. A tattoo snaked from his wrist to the knuckles of his left hand. I couldn't make out the design. His chestnut hair was slicked back, and a faint beard dusted a jawline that went on for literally forever. His blue eyes twinkled with either mischief or malice.

I didn't know which.

"The party's in back," I told him, wanting to be alone.

"I'm not here for the party."

"Oh, okay. If you're selling something, we're not interested."

He laughed and it was like listening to a hot knife cut butter. "You're very funny, Clementine. No one's told me that."

My hackles rose. "How do you know my name?"

"Because I've been wanting to talk to you about a business proposition."

Suddenly my brain fired on all cylinders. This was Sykes Laffoon's boss. This was the man who wanted to use me for his little evil mafia empire.

"No, thank you," I told him.

He smirked as if no wasn't in his vocabulary. "Don't you want to hear me out?"

"Not at all."

"Well, then." He took a step forward. The scent of his cologne trickled up my nose. He smelled of the beach—all ocean spray and salty air. "If you don't want to hear me, then I'll have to show you."

Before I could argue, this strange man snapped his fingers, and Peachwood melted away just before I was plunged into darkness.

What will happen next? Clem's adventures continue in WITCH IT OR LIST IT. You can order it HERE.

Be sure to sign up for my newsletter so that you never miss a release. Click HERE to sign up!

Plus, join my private Facebook group, the Bless Your Witch Club. There you will receive sneak peaks at books, be the first to receive special giveaway offers and watch as I interview other authors that you love. But it's only available in the club, so join HERE.

And…I love to hear from you! Please feel free to drop me a line anytime. You can email me amy@amyboylesauthor.com.

ALSO BY AMY BOYLES

SERIES READING ORDER

A MAGICAL RENOVATION MYSERY
WITCHER UPPER
RENOVATION SPELL
DEMOLITION PREMONITION
WITCHER UPPER CHRISTMAS
BARN BEWITCHMENT

LOST SOUTHERN MAGIC
(Sweet Tea Witches, Southern Belles and Spells, Southern Ghost Wrangles and Bless Your Witch Crossover)
THE GOLD TOUCH THAT WENT CATTYWAMPUS
THE YELLOW-BELLIED SCAREDY CAT
A MESS OF SIRENS
KNEE-HIGH TO A THIEF

BELLES AND SPELLS MATCHMAKER MYSTERY
DEADLY SPELLS AND A SOUTHERN BELLE
CURSED BRIDES AND ALIBIS
MAGICAL DAMES AND DATING GAMES
SOME PIG AND A MUMMY DIG

SWEET TEA WITCH MYSTERIES
SOUTHERN MAGIC
SOUTHERN SPELLS
SOUTHERN MYTHS
SOUTHERN SORCERY
SOUTHERN CURSES

SOUTHERN KARMA

SOUTHERN MAGIC THANKSGIVING

SOUTHERN MAGIC CHRISTMAS

SOUTHERN POTIONS

SOUTHERN FORTUNES

SOUTHERN HAUNTINGS

SOUTHERN WANDS

SOUTHERN CONJURING

SOUTHERN WISHES

SOUTHERN DREAMS

SOUTHERN MAGIC WEDDING

SOUTHERN OMENS

SOUTHERN JINXED

SOUTHERN BEGINNINGS

SOUTHERN GHOST WRANGLER MYSTERIES

SOUL FOOD SPIRITS

HONEYSUCKLE HAUNTING

THE GHOST WHO ATE GRITS (Crossover with Pepper and Axel from Sweet Tea Witches)

BACKWOODS BANSHEE

MISTLETOE AND SPIRITS

BLESS YOUR WITCH SERIES

SCARED WITCHLESS

KISS MY WITCH

QUEEN WITCH

QUIT YOUR WITCHIN'

FOR WITCH'S SAKE

DON'T GIVE A WITCH

WITCH MY GRITS

FRIED GREEN WITCH

SOUTHERN WITCHING

Y'ALL WITCHES

HOLD YOUR WITCHES

SOUTHERN SINGLE MOM PARANORMAL MYSTERIES

The Witch's Handbook to Hunting Vampires

The Witch's Handbook to Catching Werewolves

The Witch's Handbook to Trapping Demons

ABOUT THE AUTHOR

Hey, I'm Amy,

I write books for folks who crave laugh-out-loud paranormal mysteries. I help bring humor into readers' lives. I've got a Pharm D in pharmacy, a BA in Creative Writing and a Masters in Life.

And when I'm not writing or chasing around two small children (one of which is four going on thirteen), I can be found antique shopping for a great deal, getting my roots touched up (because that's an every four week job) and figuring out when I can get back to Disney World.

If you're dying to know more about my wacky life, here are three things you don't know about me.

—In college I spent a semester at Marvel Comics working in the X-Men office.

—I worked at Carnegie Hall.

—I grew up in a barbecue restaurant—literally. My parents owned one.

If you want to reach out to me—and I love to hear from readers—you can email me at amyboylesauthor@gmail.com.

Happy reading!